HANNAH

HANNAH

DIANA VAZQUEZ

COTEAU BOOKS

Edited by Geoffrey Ursell.

Cover painting by Dawn Pearcey.
Cover and book design by Duncan Campbell.
Printed and bound in Canada.

The publisher gratefully acknowledges the financial assistance of the Saskatchewan
Arts Board, the Canada Council for the Arts, the Department of Canadian
Heritage, and the City of Regina Arts Commission, for its publishing program.

Canadian Cataloguing in Publication Data

Vazquez, Diana, 1960 –
Hannah
ISBN 1-55050-149-6

I. Title.
PS8593.A988H35 1999   jC813'.54   C99-920025-9
PZ7.V482Ha 1999

COTEAU BOOKS
401-2206 Dewdney Ave.
Regina, Saskatchewan
Canada   S4R 1H3

AVAILABLE IN THE US FROM
General Distribution Services
85 River Rock Drive, Suite 202
Buffalo, New York, USA   1420

To my daughter Carmen,
who brings richness to life

N

ROB

MRS.
WHITBY'S

TO HALIFAX

MINE

HANNAH'S
HOUSE

Pictou County,
Nova Scotia
1858

CHAPTER ONE

HANNAH COULD HEAR THE TRAIN IN THE distance. The wind picked up the sound and made it seem as if it was coming out of the sky. The idea made her smile. She stood beside a line of ponies hooked up to coal carts which the breeze swept across, lifting veils of black dust into the air. The clearing was quiet and humid and the woods around them were thick. Dozens of mine workers stood waiting for the train, looking oddly out of place in the wilderness with their coal-blackened hands and shovels.

Grace gently gathered Hannah's hair and patted it into place behind her shoulders. Hannah pushed her sister's hands away. "Leave off! I told ya."

Grace had managed to scrub all of her sisters except Hannah who thought she was fine the way she was. Grace thought she looked like a mossy-faced beggar, but she hadn't insisted, knowing from experience that Hannah would fight with her and mess them both up.

The train swept in, breaking the quiet in the clearing, its flared iron skirt pushing through clouds of dust. The pony boys steadied their animals and men moved forward, their shovels readied. The bustle of loading coal had no sooner started than it stopped abruptly as a single passenger stepped off the train, a young woman wearing yellow. Yellow. Many of them had never seen cloth that colour. Yellow, like cream churned to butter and left to ripen, a yellow that would melt if you touched it.

The young woman's skirt fluttered in the wind as she looked around. It appeared she was standing on a small wooden stage in a clearing with a black floor and dust lifting off every surface; everything was brown and gray and everyone looked alike, stained by coal dust, wearing rough clothes made of undyed sacking, looking wild and foreign. The first surprise was over, and activity resumed in the clearing.

"Aunt Catherine!" A girl almost as tall as

Catherine with a lovely, bright face ran up the steps to the small passenger platform. She was dressed strangely in an old gown that might have been worn to a society tea in London, a fussy, outdated dress of grey silk which had been reconstructed into the style of a servant's frock but had layers of lace left on it.

"I'm so happy to see you. I'm Grace." The girl's smile was sincere, and Catherine received her hug with a sense of relief. "I'm the oldest," Grace continued, as if the commotion of the boys urging their ponies up the loading chute and the roar of coal hitting iron didn't exist. She picked up her aunt's bag and dragged it down the stairs. When they got to the bottom, she pointed to one of three girls standing together wearing simple undyed shifts. "This here is Evelyn. She doesn't hear, so don't be insulted by her if she doesn't answer. But I'm goin' out of order. After me the next oldest is - T'resa!" Grace's tone changed to a shrill cry. "Get your paws off 'a Aunt Cathrin's skirt!"

Theresa had been gently touching the fine yellow muslin, but now she clamped her plump hands around the material and yanked the skirt up with all the strength of her five-year-old arms, hoping to get a glimpse of what was suspending it in a bell shape. Hannah moved fast before they could all see what was underneath, pulling Theresa away and lifting her across her shoulder.

"I'm Hannah," She raised her hand in greeting, knowing Grace would be mute and flustered for the next moment. She always lost her composure if any little problem presented itself.

"Hello," Catherine held out a thin, gloved hand which Hannah accepted as if she were shaking a stick.

"Hope y' brought some cures." She motioned to her aunt's over-packed bag, but Catherine barely seemed to have heard what she said. Her eyes darted about the clearing; her shoulders flinched with every rumble and crash that the workers made. No point trying to talk now, Hannah decided. She turned and carried Theresa, kicking and protesting, down the road.

Grace picked up her aunt's bag and said, "They're the two wild ones. Evelyn's really sweet though." She jabbed Evelyn with her elbow.

Evelyn gave her aunt a happy wave and ran down the road after Hannah and Theresa.

CATHERINE SQUEEZED HER SKIRTS through the doorway of the shanty and stopped for a moment, adjusting to the darkness inside. Her eyes moved around the room. There was a black iron stove streaked with ashes, a plank table, and four chairs with rush seats that were coming apart. Through a doorway into a second room, she could see limp feet in the straw. She stepped into the room and suppressed a gasp. Her sister lay on a mattress of straw, her newborn baby beside her. Her breathing was shallow and fast, and her cheeks were flushed with fever.

Catherine remembered her sister Maggie as a strong, carefree young woman, who played and worked with equal vigour, a sister twelve years older who had married Angus Campbell, a dreamer with high hopes for their future. They'd moved in with Angus's uncle to help him farm a large tract of land, but a few years of bad weather and ruined crops had brought them near starvation.

They'd left Scotland and come to Nova Scotia with a boat load of other farmers and settlers who had little to lose. In all the years that Catherine had been separated from her sister, she had never imagined that Maggie lived in such hardship. Her face crumpled, but she saw the four girls watching her, dismay darkening their faces, and she stopped herself from crying.

"It's a lucky thing," Catherine started to say, wanting to give the girls something positive, "...a lucky thing, really...that, that it's summer and she's warm."

"She's burnin' up with fever," Hannah pointed out.

"Yes, but it would be worse in the winter," Catherine maintained. "Now let's have a cup of tea – or a drink of water," she added, seeing them glance at each other.

"We've a bit of tea," Grace explained. "I can make you a cup if you like, or you can have it another day."

"I'll have it today, please," said Catherine.

Grace made her aunt tea, using the last few leaves in the tin, and they sat around her while she drank it.

"Has your mother been sleeping long?" Catherine asked.

No one answered. A small mirror was in Grace's hands. Each of the girls had taken a turn gazing into it before Grace had taken it back, and now they all watched her examine herself. Catherine smiled at their wonder over the mirror and pulled out another gift, a diary she placed in Hannah's hands. Hannah ran her hands over its cloth cover and flipped through its blank pages, then let it fall from her fingers onto the ground. Catherine felt her face go red, but tried not to show how offended she was. She turned to Grace. "Has your mother been unwell for long?"

Grace lowered the mirror but kept her eyes on her own reflection. "For a bit."

"Has the doctor seen her?"

Grace's eyes flickered up. "There's no doctor."

"Has anyone seen her?"

"Just you," Hannah said, disappointed. She had expected her mother's younger sister to be someone who could take care of things, someone like her mother with a strong back and capable hands. She thought of the light, bony squeeze of her aunt's fingers when she'd taken her hand. She was going to be as useless as her gifts, gleaming with newness but good for nothing.

Hannah watched as Catherine pulled a painted doll out of her bag. Evelyn and Theresa were captured by its delicate beauty and fine lace dress. Catherine placed the doll in Evelyn's arms. Theresa's lips trembled, then tightened in an angry line, and she grabbed a handful of the doll's fine white hair and pulled it towards her. She and Evelyn struggled ferociously for the doll until Hannah rescued it from their tug of war. She held it up in the air, a clump of its hair missing, one eye rolling askew, and put her hand on Theresa's head to hold her down while she handed it to Evelyn. Theresa started to cry.

"Look, I have a gift for you too," Catherine brought out a small cradle with lace-edged blankets, a cradle just the right size for Evelyn's doll. There was a moment of silence when Theresa saw her gift. No one moved except Catherine, who reached out with a handkerchief to dab at Theresa's tears. Theresa slapped her hand away and hurled the cradle against the wall where a rocker splintered off.

"What'd you bring this rot for?" Hannah demanded abruptly, kicking the diary across the floor. She was surprised to see her aunt sink slightly in her chair. She usually received a clout on the ear for her outbursts.

"I...I thought since Evelyn and Theresa are only a few years apart they could play together with the doll and cradle...." Catherine let her sentence fall away.

Hannah tossed the broken cradle into a sack. She tugged at Theresa's tangled hair. "Robbie'll glue it up. All right T'resa? Stop your wailing." Theresa had slumped on the ground. Hannah nudged her with her foot. "Come on, it's still light out. Walk with me." Theresa folded her head into her arms and cried louder.

Hannah picked up the sack and stepped outside. It was almost the end of August. Orange sunlight fell across the rows of shacks that spread out from the rail yard and the mine. Nearer the train station, away from the miners' quarters, were two large, fine homes which belonged to the supervisor and an engineer from the company. Down the road, the new church was being built and nearby it was Robbie's wood shop. If she hurried, she could get there before he sat down to his tea. Hannah's dark hair fell into her eyes. She shook it away and scrambled along the path.

Robbie's shop stank from the pot of glue he kept on the back of the stove. Hannah called it pony glue because that was where the mining ponies ended up after they collapsed in the tunnels. She set the broken cradle on his work bench. He put aside his chisel and whistled, admiring the fine toy.

"It's T'resa's. She hates it."

"How's that?" Robbie asked.

"Aunt Catherine brung it. She's up from Halifax to help with the baby while Ma gets better."

Robbie nodded. He'd seen the procession of Campbell girls accompany the young woman, barely an adult herself, through the settlement. She'd created a stir, stopped the men in their tracks, some staring with open mouths when she'd held her skirts up to her ankles to avoid the mud on the road, displaying white shoes with dozens of tiny buttons closing over her ankles.

"The problem is...she's...fancy," Hannah continued.

"And?"

"And not good for anything."

"She's just come, Hannah."

"She won't last."

"Give her time." Robbie picked up the broken

rocker, thinking she probably wouldn't. There weren't many women in the mining settlement, and those who lived here struggled to make homes with few supplies and no comforts. "Let's have a look at this." Robbie stirred the clear yellow glue and let a stream run off the brush. "I've got some apples in the back. They're a bit brown, but take 'em. They'll cook up sweet." He brushed glue on the broken pieces of wood.

Hannah left the cradle at Robbie's shop, clamped to dry overnight, and hurried home with the apples. The sun was gone, and cooking fires from the miners' shacks flickered in the deep blue dusk. In the distance she could see the furnaces at the coal mine. Her breath caught in her throat for a moment as she saw the silhouette of her father standing on the path home. Her eyes watered and she tried to focus on him, but he dissolved in her watery gaze. She often thought she saw him.

When Hannah got home a fire burned in the stove and her aunt was trimming a meat pie. Theresa was under the table with Evelyn's doll. Evelyn was outside on the back porch sitting in the empty washtub, tapping the sides with her spoon, excited by the food she'd seen her aunt unpack. She had no hearing but that didn't make her quiet. Her hands were always touching and tapping while she made noises in her throat. Their mother said she was trying to find her voice.

Hannah put the apples on the table. "From Robbie down at the carpentry shop. He bids y' welcome."

"Thanks," Catherine smiled, her cheeks were pink from the heat of the stove. Hannah found herself smiling back, but she pinched the corners of her mouth down so that her smile was not too welcoming.

She stepped into the doorway of the room where her mother lay. Her clothes were twisted as if she'd dropped to sleep in the middle of a spell. Hannah straightened her dress and covered her up. She noticed her lips were dry. Winnie, her baby sister, was red and tiny beside her.

Catherine cooked the apples with the meat pie, and when she brought them to the table their skins were bursting with juice. The first slice into the pie released a cloud of steam. The aroma made Hannah light-headed. Theresa grabbed her aunt's wrist and roughly guided the first serving to her bowl. Catherine quickly served the others and watched as her nieces put their hands in their bowls and scooped food onto their spoons and into their mouths, sucking the gravy off their fingers, swallowing almost without chewing.

Theresa set her bowl down, licked clean. "Did you bring more?"

"I brought supplies" Catherine hesitated, "for the week."

"For only one week?" Grace sat up.

"Then what'll we eat?" demanded Theresa.

"Well...I...I have a position that I can't leave in Halifax and...I'll talk with your mother once she's up." Catherine looked at the shocked faces around the table. Theresa began to cry.

Hannah pushed her chair back and collected the bowls. "I knew it. Shush T'resa. Go get some water an' get Ev'lyn t' help you carry."

Theresa wailed while she picked up the water pail and banged it in front of Evelyn. Catherine winced. Her head throbbed from the constant noise in the tiny shack. In the other room, her leather bag gleamed like well-polished livery against the hay where Hannah had tossed it. The thought of sleeping in the airless room, that smelled of damp earth and old straw, with four unwashed children, a weak newborn, and her ailing sister made her feel sick. She brought her hand up to her ear as Theresa continued banging on the water pail.

"Stop that racket and get going!" Grace snapped. She took Catherine's hand and stroked it. "Do y' want me to sing you a song?"

Hannah stepped outside. She set the bowls in the washtub and watched the hills while she waited for the water. She could hear Grace practice her voice scales inside. Grace was the one who was coddled, who was sent to visit the mine supervisor's wife. She was the one who used to sing for their father after his bath every night. She was showing off, Hannah thought, listening to her voice swoop and trill.

IT WAS DARK when Catherine stepped outside, where Hannah was crouched at the edge of the stoop. Hannah looked down at her aunt's shoes and wondered how a person could have such dainty feet. Her own feet were already wider than her aunt's.

14

"May I plait your hair?" Catherine asked.

"What for?"

"Doesn't it bother you?"

"No."

"I think it would look nice." She picked up a few strands of hair. Hannah shook her head and Catherine let the strands fall away. "Grace and I were planning how to care for your mother."

"There's no one else t' do it but me."

"In Halifax there are places where she could be cared for and –"

"Top or bottom?"

"Pardon me?"

"Top or bottom ? Where'll y' sleep?"

"What? I...I don't know what you mean."

"Y' can sleep over our heads or along our feet. Door's closer if y' lie by our feet."

"I'll sleep in the other room."

"There's no bedding there."

Catherine pursed her lips. She did not consider straw to be bedding. "Grace told me it would be difficult for you to leave. I'm only telling you."

"We're not going, not one of us. We're not." She wasn't going to leave matters in the hands of someone who looked all light and airy like a flower gone to seed.

Catherine felt her mouth tighten. "You can't stay here."

"Yes, I can."

"No, you can't."

"I can."

Catherine caught herself before she said, *You can't.* She was the authority here after all. "Once your mother's better she'll collect all of you," she said in her calmest, most confident voice.

"Collect us where?"

"From the place I find for you. I didn't realize she was so ill or I would have made arrangements before coming, but the letter she wrote me is from almost a month ago and she didn't mention anything."

"Why would she?"

"Because I am her sister and her only surviving family," Catherine's voice was strained. "And I will do what I think is best whether you want me to or not." Mosquitoes were coming out of the forest, and she slapped one off her neck.

"Send us to a work house?"

"Find you a home – some place where you'll go to school and learn something!" Catherine couldn't understand why Hannah didn't want to go to Halifax. They'd have beds and knives and forks and plates. They'd have proper clothes and even perhaps music lessons.

"I already know lots. I already know more 'n you." Hannah stood up and tossed a stone into a thicket. A bird flew into the air. The blur of its wings beating in the dark startled Catherine. She looked at Hannah but could only see the glimmer of her eyes, like water at night hiding what lies below the surface. "I know how to find food." Hannah looked down at the high-heeled shoes that encased her aunt's feet. "Can you?"

Catherine was tired and wanted to go inside. "Hannah, she'll die here."

Hannah didn't answer. One spring day she had seen a cow slip down the bank of a river and into the rushing current. A group of men had flung a rope around its neck and tried to pull it out, but the cow had leaned back and resisted the rescue. She remembered the farmer cursing and crying while water curled around the cow's udder and up over its back. Hannah felt like she was in fast-moving water too. She felt like a dumb beast, not daring to lift a foot and weaken the foundation she stood on lest she be swept away. "How'll you take her without killin' her?"

Catherine looked at Hannah, surprised. Yes, it was possible her sister was too sick to move. "I don't know," she pulled her shawl around her head and fanned away clouds of mosquitoes. But what would they do if that were the case?

Hannah spoke as if she had read her aunt's thoughts. "Elsie Fraser'll take Winnie. She's already feeding one, she'll put Winnie on the other tit. She tol' me she would."

Hannah stood and poured the wash water on the ground. "Somethin'll turn up for us, anyway," she said, not knowing what. The important thing was to stay here where they had friends, where people knew them and would help them – at least until their mother was better.

CHAPTER TWO

HANNAH SAW GRACE STANDING AT THE threshold of the hut and yelled, "Get Ma some tea. She's lyin' there pantin'."

"Stop orderin' me!" Grace entered reluctantly. She didn't want to be inside where it was dark and quiet and her mother lay so still she could have been a bale of hay in the room scattered with straw.

Hannah brushed past her. "'Bout time you were back." She stood in the doorway and closed her eyes, feeling the sun on her face.

"Sweet dreams?"

Hannah opened her eyes and saw a thin boy her own age with light, watchful eyes. "Hello, Gregory."

"You're white like a plastered wall. Not sick are y'?" He wasn't used to her being so still and worn looking. She shook her head. "Come for a walk then?"

Wind combed the grass on the hillsides in one direction, brushing Hannah's ankles as she strolled with Gregory up to the woods where she had first seen him a year ago. Hannah had hidden and watched him chewing on bits of bark. He'd spat out a piece of birch bark and moved on to a maple tree, a beech tree, and then an oak, tasting each one. From the other side of the bush, Scotty Mackay and his four brothers had also watched and when Gregory had begun picking at the bark of a fir tree, Scotty had pulled out his knife and walked up to him.

"Let me help y' lad. This one's tasty." He cut a circle around the trunk, pulling away a ring of bark.

"Is that the one made of sugar?" Gregory had asked.

Scotty's brothers rolled out of the bushes laughing. Gregory turned to leave, but Scotty caught his shirt and tackled him to the ground. "Wait a min'te. I'll get y' some sugar from the candy tree."

Hannah hadn't waited to see how much bark the Mackay brothers would stuff in the new boy's mouth. She loaded an acorn in her sling shot and hit Scotty in the ear. He cried out in pain. She reloaded quickly and caught his brother, Charlie, in the chest, then aimed again for Scotty, knowing if he left, they'd all leave. Scotty had withstood four more acorns, cursing and looking in the tangled wood to find his attacker before he had left, shouting a warning at the trees.

Hannah had retreated too, knowing the Mackay brothers would be back looking for revenge. She hadn't seen Gregory again for months. His father and older brother entered the mines the day after they arrived, and Gregory had been sent to work for a family gathering its harvest. He hadn't come back to the mining camp until the fields were picked clean for winter.

The next time Hannah met him was in February, when he opened the door to their shanty and quickly let himself in, shivering and shaking snow off his clogs. He was wearing summer clothes and a wool scarf wound around his neck. The scarf trailed over one shoulder. "Hello," he said. He looked around the room shyly, nodding towards Hannah and Evelyn, who were dipping candles together.

"Hello Gregory," Grace stood up. "How's your mother?"

"She's suffering with the cold. We all are."

"I've put aside a few things for you." Grace was

doing her charity work, Hannah could tell by the voice she used. She was proud to be Mrs. Whitby's representative in the settlement, since the mine supervisor's wife was frightened by the miners' quarters and wouldn't go near them. "An' I spoke to the Frasers on the other side. They've some supplies for you as well. Tell your ma there's enough grease here to make candles for a fortnight, and we've some wool for you." It was customary for families, little as they had, to round up supplies to help new settlers over the first winter.

"That's grand."

"I'll find something for you to carry it in," Grace smiled.

"I'll get it," Hannah said quickly. She went out back and got a sap pail, put the fat in the bottom, and tied the wool to the handle. While she worked she noticed that the boy didn't scrape his feet and blush around Grace like most boys did. She handed him the pail. "There y' go. Bring the pail back in three weeks when we go collectin' sugar from the trees." She watched him.

"Aye," he said with an air of experience, "that's when the sap'll be runnin'."

Hannah's eyes narrowed. "How'd you know that?"

The two measured each other. "That's what I've been told," Gregory said slowly.

"Hope y' find somethin' sweeter this time," Hannah grinned.

Gregory flushed. "It wasn't too bad...as...as I had a friend along." He nodded at her. "Ta."

"It's all right," Hannah laughed. "You're not the first one's come here thinkin' there's trees made of sugar."

Hannah smiled at the memory, as she and Gregory settled on a ridge of rocks. Gregory traced letters in the ground with a stick. R-I-G-H-T. "Look at this Hannah, what d'ye make of this?"

Hannah glanced at the letters. "Looks a jumble."

"Aye, looks it. But see this G an' H here?" Gregory pointed with his stick. He liked teaching Hannah the little that he knew of reading and writing. "Y' don't speak 'em. They're silent. See, this here's the word right."

"Right," Hannah repeated, looking at the scars on Gregory's hands when he underlined the letters G and H. She looked down the hill at the cluster of huts below. She didn't know how long her family had been here. Maybe four years. They'd arrived in April, 1854, she knew, because a group of settlers had ended up at the mine and they often talked about the hard journey over.

The miners' shanties had been put up quickly, with green wood which warped as it dried, leaving gaps in the walls that were filled with moss and mud. The clearing around the shanties was full of tree stumps which had been left in the ground, because it took half a day to take out one stump and the company was busy pushing back the forest in little plots to make room for newcomers. The few women who lived in the settlement planted their kitchen gardens between the stumps and roots. Closer to the mine, two long, low buildings had been built side by side. They were called the barracks and were home to unmarried men or miners waiting for a shanty, who bunked down in a line and stored their possessions underneath their cots.

Gregory put his stick down. "What's eatin' you, Hannah?"

"Everything." Her aunt Catherine had left a week ago. She had shown them how to keep their mother's forehead cool and how to get spoonfuls of liquid between her lips. She had cooked and played games and slept with them in the straw.

And, now that she was gone, Hannah discovered that everything was harder than it had looked when her aunt had done it. Water ran down her mother's chin when she tried to give her a drink, and she could barely shift her around so she didn't get sores from lying in one place. Their food supplies were low, and Grace was at Mrs. Whitby's most of the time.

"Ma's not gettin' better. I feel like I'm just sittin' there watchin' her, doin' no good."

Gregory pursed his lips and tried to think of something that would make Hannah feel better.

"Besides," she went on, "there's no one to work." Her father used to boast that he was rich with daughters and wouldn't have even one of them changed into a boy. Just one boy would have been good, Hannah thought. Just one to go into the mine so they would have credit at the company store, so their rent would be paid.

"If there was any way I could help y'...." Gregory's voice trailed off. Hannah watched his fingers trace over the letters, gouging them into the earth. Her own hands were sturdier than his, toughened from the bite of the coal bucket handle across her palm, from carrying water from the stream and pounding clothes. Hannah tensed the muscles in her back. She was fit enough to be a miner, yes she was. And she knew enough about the mines too.

"Greg'ry," Hannah paused. Her mouth was suddenly dry. "I know one way."

"T' help?"

"Aye."

"What?"

"It's...."

"What?"

"I take your place in the mine."

"It won't work, Hannah."

Hannah jumped to her feet.

"Sit down, silly. I'll hear y' out but I'm tellin' you – don't get your hopes up for this scheme."

Hannah crouched before Gregory. "It's dark as pitch in the morning when you go in – if I pull my cap down over my face and go to your place – I know you're a breaker boy – no one'll ever know. You just tell me where your spot is."

"It changes."

"Then I'll go where they send me."

"D'you know what it's like?"

"Where'll we go, Gregory? No one'll want us.

Not with Evelyn the way she is. Not with Theresa. Not with me."

"It's horrible in there," Gregory insisted.

"It doesn't matter. Look at my hands," Hannah punched her hand and held it out. "I'll sort more coal than you. Maybe even double. I'll share my pay with you."

Gregory stood up. His face was suddenly red. "Think I'll let you pay me to be idle?"

"Do it for just one day. Just so's I can see if I can do it."

"An' what'll I do?"

"You can teach Evelyn and Theresa their letters."

"I'm not a teacher!"

"You're more a teacher than a miner! I heard say you're so pitiful they'd almost be better off without you!" The men called him *lily white* because his hands never hardened; they were cut by rocks and blistered by the work. His thin shoulders trembled if he had to lift a shovel full of coal or pull a tub up to a pony. "Just for one day, Gregory."

Gregory's eyes glowed with pain. His voice trembled. "No, Hannah."

"A short try. Nothing more."

"My cousin John's come in at Pictou last week.

He goes in with me every day."

"I can do it."

"It's impossible."

"It's not!" He wasn't going to help her. She wanted to punch him. Instead, she spun around and ran down the hill.

Gregory called after her. "You know what happens if a girl goes in the mines. There'll be a disaster – a cave in – a–"

"Miners' superstitions!" Hannah shouted over her shoulders. The woods picked up the words and flung them back at her as she bounded down the hill.

CHAPTER THREE

"HANNAH...." SWEAT BEADED HER MOTHER'S forehead and her chest rose and fell rapidly. "Get me up, love, I need a walk around."

"Maybe y' need some water, Ma."

"I need a walk around." Hannah looked at her mother's face and wondered if she saw anything through her glassy eyes. She helped her up and they took a few steps together, but her mother lost her strength and slouched against her. Hannah stumbled and buckled under her weight.

"Grace," Hannah called when she heard the front door open. There was no answer. "Grace, come an' help me." Hannah struggled to support her mother. "Ev'lyn?" she called, though she knew Evelyn wouldn't hear. Who else would it be? Hannah strained her thin arms to lay her mother down. She covered her and went to the door. A tall youth with sandy coloured hair and grey eyes was there, and behind him, looking miserable, stood Gregory.

"Didn't y' hear?"

"Hannah...." Gregory started.

"I've come t' tell y' t' leave," the tall youth interrupted abruptly. He was older than her, but not much, perhaps fourteen years old, like Grace.

"What?"

"Y're to be out by morning."

"Who'll make us?" Hannah didn't believe that anyone would throw them out. Not anyone who knew her father. They'd all come to his funeral and said it had been an honour to know him.

Theresa crawled out from under the table where she had been playing with Evelyn's doll. She grabbed Hannah's tunic and clung to her legs. "Get off, Theresa." Hannah pushed her away in case she needed her legs for kicking.

"If you're not out, we'll move y' out."

"Says who?" demanded Hannah.

"Says the company manager. There's a miner waitin' for a place."

"As long as we pay, what difference is it if we're miners or not?"

"Y' haven't paid," the youth snapped.

Hannah went to the stove and took a small tin from behind it which she emptied into her hand and held out to the youth.

Gregory stepped up to the door. "Put away your money, Hannah. We'll work it out with the manager. We'll ask for more time. Eh, John?" He nudged his cousin's elbow.

Hannah ignored Gregory and kept her hand out, money on her open palm. As John reached to take it, she flung it out the door. "There, go pick it up."

John flushed, but without another word he stepped outside and gathered the money.

"The manager sent him. He didn't ask to do this," Gregory said sadly as Hannah closed the door in his face.

A moment later, Grace came in. "What's all that money lyin' about outside?"

"It's the rent," Hannah didn't look at her sister.

"Where's it from?"

"It's your turn t' stay with Ma."

Grace grabbed Hannah's arm. "Where'd y' get it?"

"From our savings," Hannah answered sarcastically.

Grace's face whitened. "You didn't throw away

our passage fares to Halifax, did y'? You did! You just threw away everything Aunt Catherine left us!" Her voice was strained.

"We've a place t' sleep at least."

"We were supposed t' leave in a fortnight. You promised Aunt Catherine," Grace yelled. "You promised! You broke your word."

"I couldn't keep my word!" Hannah's lips trembled. "I only meant we'd go if Ma was all right. I didn't promise we'd leave no matter what."

"What'll we do now?" Grace flopped down on a chair and buried her face in her hands. "What'll we do?"

Grace cried a long time, and Hannah was relieved when she finally calmed down to a quiet gloom as evening approached. There was a feeling of calamity in the house that was worse than anything she remembered. Evelyn looked scared and confused and stayed so closely by Hannah that they kept bumping into each other.

While Catherine had been there, Theresa had sat under the bare hoops of her skirt which had been hung in a corner as there had been no room in the shanty for her great wide skirt. Theresa had draped flowers and wild grasses on the wooden hoops and sat inside singing and playing house. Now Theresa took refuge under the table, silently curled into a ball.

Hannah picked the last cobs of corn from the garden and pulled the stalks out of the ground. They would make kindling when they dried. She surveyed the garden to see what was left to harvest. A bit of squash and some potatoes. Maybe a week or two worth of food. After a small supper, Hannah took the bowls outside. She crouched beside the wash basin and swished them out, trailing her hands in the water, thinking of nothing. Footsteps in the dark made her look around.

"Hannah...." It was Gregory whispering her name.

"What d' you want?"

"Shhh," Gregory slipped nervously onto the porch and crouched in the shadows against the back wall. "I've changed my mind."

Hannah looked at him. His thin white arms gleamed like bones in the dark. "Changed your mind?"

"I'll let y' take my place. Just for a day though."

Hannah's heart jumped.

"D'y still want t' do it?" Gregory asked, watching her.

Hannah nodded.

"I just hope what they say about girls in mines isn't true," Gregory smiled nervously.

"It'll be all right." Hannah spoke in a high, soft voice that was unlike her, and Gregory realized that she was as frightened as he was.

Gregory whispered instructions. "Start at five o'clock, finish at seven. One hour for breakfast at nine o'clock an' one for dinner at one. The men'll run out for a sip of rum during the breaks. Keep your food pail close by an' eat wherever you're working. I'll get my lantern with John an' stand in line t' be searched for matches or candles – they're not allowed 'cause of the gases."

Hannah nodded. She knew this from her father.

"You'll be dressed with your cap low an' your hair hid. Get into the yard with a group of 'em. When you slip in the gate, keep to the left. The right side's where they hand out the lanterns and count the men. John an' I go to the entrance together. Then he heads off to where he works. I'll go in for a bit, then walk back out like I've forgotten something. When you see me go out, you walk in an' take my place. No one'll know it's not me. Mind the lanterns though. Don't let anyone put one to your face." He pulled a small bundle of soot-stained clothes out from under his shirt. "I got these out of the wash. Hope my Ma doesn't miss them. Take care with them – I only have the two sets of clothes. But it's just for a day, right Hannah?"

Hannah nodded, grabbed the bundle, and stuffed it under her tunic.

HANNAH SLIPPED OUT while it was dark and found a sheltered spot in the woods. She had told Grace she would be gone in the morning to look for harvest work. She changed, sliding her legs into pants for the first time, tied her hair in a knot on the top of her head, pulled her cap low, and buttoned the thin jacket up under her chin. She folded and hid her tunic, then crouched low and waited.

The morning mist was cold, and she shivered as she sat watching the settlement from the hills. The women were up already, she could tell by the cooking fires reflected in the windows. Then, as if a silent bell had rung, she saw a stream of men leave the barracks and pass under the yellow light of a lantern outside. They were joined on the road by men and boys coming out of the shanties. As if a floodgate had been opened, the roads were suddenly full of silent figures moving towards the mine, their drab clothes matching the dark morning sky. Hannah crept along beside them, hidden in the hills.

Close to the mines, she slid down to the road and entered the crowd of miners. She waited for a hand to come down on her shoulder or a cry of recognition, but the men were looking beyond her at the hole cut in the hillside. Hannah stayed to the left of a cluster of men at the gate. On the right, as Gregory had said, was a small hut where two men stood. One called out numbers as he handed out lanterns, picks and shovels and the other recorded them in a ledger. Hannah made herself walk steadily, though she wanted to fall on her stomach and slither behind a line of ponies waiting to be led into the mine.

The men pressed together and stooped automatically at the mouth of the tunnel as rock walls closed over their heads. Shoulders pushed in against hers and food pails banged her legs. She was swept along with the miners, not knowing where Gregory was. What would she do if she reached the bottom without finding him?

Somewhere ahead of her she heard a commotion. It was Gregory calling out apologies. Miners swatted him on the head and pushed him as he fought against their tide. All of a sudden, he appeared out of the grey press of bodies and stumbled against her. She pushed him away roughly as the others had done, their hands met, and he slipped the handle of his lantern into her fingers. Their eyes flashed towards each other and then he was gone, apologizing and explaining he'd forgotten his dinner pail. Relief made her weak.

The tunnel sloped down, and the ground was scored with uneven ruts and cart rails. She felt the rhythm of the miners, and her body took on the same cadence. The air grew warm as they travelled deeper into the mines. The tunnel opened into a room, supported by pillars of coal. The walls were ragged and black, filled with pick marks and holes. Hannah hesitated, looking to see where to go. She saw Wilbur Mackay who was close to her age, perhaps a bit older, head for an opening to the right, and, knowing that she must look as if she belonged, she followed him. She stopped in her tracks as a voice boomed behind her.

"Goin' for a picnic, Gregory Graham?" Hannah

turned around. "Y've got your food pail. Now get to your place," She saw the underground manager incline his head towards a small opening.

Hannah stepped back from the light of his lantern and hurried to the opening hidden behind a pillar of coal, aware of the manager's eyes on her back. The opening did not lead to a tunnel, but to a low space cut out of the wall where there was a wooden chute filled with rock and coal. There was barely enough room to sit up straight, which was why the smallest boys worked there. She hunched on a wooden plank laid across the chute.

Hannah tried to remember what her father had told her about coal. It had a black sparkle to it. She was careful to keep her face to her work. Her hands sorted fluidly. Her eyes were always one step ahead of her fingers, choosing the next stones to flick aside for the slag heaps outside. She worked with an ease that was dangerously unlike Gregory's fumbling, halting work. John, sent with a team to break into a new seam in the west tunnel, slowed down as he passed, and watched.

At nine o'clock the breakfast bells rang. Shadowy streams of men walked through the dark. After they had passed and the tunnels grew quiet, Hannah was still sorting, caught in the rhythm of her work. The lonely noise of her rocks clacking against each other pulled her out of her reverie. Her eyes flicked up under her cap. The other boys were sitting by their food pails, potatoes or bread in hand, looking at her with a stillness and concentration that made her stop immediately. She pulled her pail over. If one of them picked up a lantern and shone it in her face, she'd be discovered. Hannah ate her potato, keeping her eyes on her feet. She must do nothing out of place. It took a while for her heart to slow down and her breathing to return to normal.

When the work whistle sounded again, Hannah lingered for a moment, trying to think how Gregory would act. She couldn't be herself, bursting to make a living, she had to be Gregory with soft hands. She slowed down her sorting, pausing every once in a while. Connor Fraser, who worked behind her, leaned forward, "I thought y' were possessed. Gave me the shivers." Death came quickly and unexpectedly in the mines and anything unusual was met with fear. It could be a sign that trouble was on its way.

Hannah didn't turn around. She blew on her hands as if they were sore and shrugged her shoulders. Connor laughed and skipped a piece of rock onto the chute. The other boys who had paused for a moment to watch also relaxed, seeing the same old Gregory.

The closing bell sounded from above and the miners took up the call, relaying it to the men working deep under the hill. Hannah stood and straightened her cramped legs. Her back ached from hunching over the chute. She reached down slowly to pick up her food pail. The other boys scrambled out of the chute and up the tunnel to meet the fresh night air.

John had held back from the men coming out of the tunnels to watch his cousin. Something was wrong with him. The stiffness in his body and the quick, feverish way he'd worked in the morning were not normal. He was reminded of the sudden illness that had afflicted his parents on the journey across the Atlantic. It made him uneasy. He saw his cousin move into the crowd of men and followed.

Hannah knew she had to get outside quickly so that Gregory could step in her place before John came out. The crush of men leaving would cover the switch. Hannah quickened her step. She darted in and out of the miners, skipping over cart rails.

As she passed Scotty Mackay, her food pail banged his. He reached out and pulled at the back of her shirt, ready to swing her around. Hannah turned her face away, balled her hand into a fist and threw it towards his face. Scotty ducked, but her knuckles grazed his cheek. He grabbed the back of her neck and pushed her head down.

"Who do y' think y' are hittin' out at me with your scrawny hands?" He squeezed her neck hard, talking to the back of her head. "I'll have t' teach y' a lesson, lily white, won't I?" Scotty pulled her along by the scruff of her neck. The opening of the tunnel appeared ahead of them. Hannah pushed her feet into the ground to brake Scotty's uphill lope. He raised his arm to cuff her in the ear, but John had caught up with them and pushed his arm back.

Hannah stumbled on her hands and knees in the scuffle that followed. Men passed with rough calls and hoots. Scotty's father, Mac, a man with coal-lined wrinkles covering his face and a thin mouth that looked like a cut, snarled. "Take it outside, boys. No fightin' in the mine."

Scotty and John pushed away from each other. John picked Hannah up and set her on her feet. He bent and looked under her cap to make sure his cousin was unharmed. When he saw Hannah's face, he drew in a sharp breath. Over his shoulder he said to Scotty, "I'll deal w't y' later."

"I'll be waitin'," Scotty answered, but he didn't press the fight. John came from a clan of stern, bull-chested men, the kind he didn't like to take on even if they were newcomers.

John's hand clamped down on Hannah's shoulder as he led her outside. When Gregory saw them from his hiding place, his knees buckled and he had such a coughing fit that he had to crawl away.

John led Hannah out of the gates and up the hill. After he'd tramped through the woods a while without speaking, he stopped and whirled her around. They were in a humid tangle of forest. "Who do y' think y' are?!"

"You're not my da'. You're not my ma'."

"Y' look stupid like that!" He pointed to her pants.

"I can work faster 'n all of 'em," Hannah said emphatically.

"No y' can't, because it's not your place. Putting on a pair of pants doesn't make y' fit for it."

"I'm as steady as the next," she insisted.

"Y' can't be relied on. You're a liar."

"You're the lowest yourself, you are. How many people did y' turn out?' Hannah forced herself to remain still though mosquitoes were biting her.

"None. 'Cause everyone's working where they should be."

"I have a family t' take care of," Hannah shouted.

"Everyone's carin' for someone. I fend for my brother, but nobody does what you did."

"You don't have to!" she yelled.

"Take in some mending then," John's face was set with contempt. Mosquitoes were alighting on his eyelids, his cheeks and neck.

"You're thick as mud. You don't know a-"

"I don't want to know!" He cut her off. "And don't let me catch you tryin' that again. Now get out of here." He hit his head in fury. It felt like his skin was burning, it had been stung so many times.

"I'll do what I want!" Hannah stomped away, then stopped and turned around. "D'you hear me? I'll do what I want."

"Aye. If you want a good beatin'...." He stepped towards her threateningly.

Hannah ran into the woods, shouting back at him, "I'll do what I want!"

Chapter Four

GRACE LED EVELYN ALONG THE ROAD
towards Mrs. Whitby's house, which she
could see on the hill, its slate roofs reflecting the
sun in luminous green gold swaths. Clouds of dirt
curled at their feet, and the September winds
pushed against the back of their heads. Grace wore
her hair coiled under a hat she clamped firmly
down on her head. "Ev'lyn, hold your hair together. It's gettin' into a mess again." She glanced at
her sister, unhappy with how she looked. Her
tunic was woven with different shades of undyed
wool, and her feet, which had for once been clean
when they left the shanty, were already coated with
dust up to the ankle.

The invitation to the tea party had been a surprise,
and what was even more unexpected was that Mrs.
Whitby had asked that Evelyn come with Grace.

When they reached Mrs. Whitby's door, Grace said, "Remember, be still an' don't touch my throat while I'm singin'." Grace pulled Evelyn's chin up. "Don't touch my neck," she repeated. Evelyn nodded her understanding. She wanted to go beyond the white door, where something smelled delicious.

Grace tapped the brass knocker, and the door was opened by a maid who led them to a room where Mrs. Whitby paced anxiously.

"Hello Mrs. Whitby. I hope we haven't come early." Grace took care with her pronunciation.

"You're in good time. There are few things to be arranged, and I wanted to meet your sister before the guests arrived and have her settled in...."

"You don't have to fuss with her, she'll stay where I tell her."

"So you...communicate, do you?"

"Yes, ma'am."

"Good. She can help you arrange the flowers. I'd like them placed in vases around the room – the owner's wife has come from England with her sis-ter. They'll stay here for two days before going to Halifax." Mrs. Whitby was anxious to make a good impression on her long-awaited guests. She was starving for the company of people who understood her world. In this settlement created around the mine, hers was the only house that was like a fine town home in London, furnished with brocade cushions, heavy velvet drapes, and satin covered furniture.

The miners lived in wild surroundings, and Mrs. Whitby feared that anyone living in such quarters was closer to beast than man – and animals were unpredictable; they acted on hunger and instinct, not reason and social order. Grace was an exception, a startling exception that left her wondering how such a lovely girl could be born from such base surroundings.

She turned to Grace, who looked quite acceptable in the old but barely used frock she had given her. "Should we use the violets? I don't have enough roses in bloom. Or should we make nosegays? There might be a lily of the valley or two...."

She led them through glass doors without waiting for an answer. They stood in a large room with a polished piano at one end. "We'll move in here after our tea. The chairs need arranging. And then we'll have Mrs. Sutherland's daughter, Jenny, play the piano. When she's finished, we'll present your

sister and you may sing us a song, Grace – one of
your pretty ballads. Your sister may wait in here
during the tea. After you've finished the flowers
send her into the kitchen for a piece of cake. And
do make nosegays. I think there's some lavender
too."

"Thank you, Mrs. Whitby,"

"You'll help Molly serve, won't you?"

Grace flushed. "Yes, ma'am." She wasn't invited
to tea after all.

Grace led Evelyn to a glass house which was
warm and humid inside. On a line of benches
were pots of violets and primroses – spring flowers
unfurling their buds in autumn. Evelyn copied
Grace, placing delicate sprays of flowers in
coloured glass bottles. When they were finished,
they put the nosegays in the reception room, then
Grace left Evelyn by the fire in the kitchen while
she went to keep Mrs. Whitby company.

The cook cut Evelyn a warm slice of apple cake. It
had a thick crust sprinkled with sugar and was the
most delicious thing she'd eaten in her life. Seconds
were not offered, and Evelyn picked up her plate
and licked it, keeping her eye on the cook who cut
two more apple cakes and arranged them on a large

platter which she kept out of Evelyn's reach until a maid carried it out of the heavy wood doors.

Grace came in and cleaned sugar off Evelyn's cheeks and led her to the music room. "Sit quietly here. We'll be in soon." Grace pushed her hands in the air towards Evelyn and down to the chair to signal what she meant. Evelyn nodded and repeated the hand gesture. Satisfied, Grace left to help Molly bring the tea service into the parlor.

Evelyn looked at the piano across the room and wondered what it was. Through the glass doors she could see the women in the other room. She adjusted herself in her seat and raised an imaginary cup to her mouth as the women did. Her toes curled back and forth, feeling the soft pile of the carpet. The women all laughed at once. Gauzy handkerchiefs fluttered suddenly in their hands and were raised to their mouths. Evelyn fluttered her fingers in the air and touched her lips. She took a sip from her pretend cup. She was excited and rubbed her feet together, leaving a scattering of dust beneath her chair. The women finished eating and re-arranged themselves gracefully in their seats. Evelyn positioned herself in the same way, her head up, her back confident.

When Mrs. Whitby opened the glass doors to the music room, Evelyn met the women with her legs crossed and chin up, her hands balancing an imaginary cup and saucer. There was a collective breath drawn in and a quiet pause filled the room. Mrs. Whitby looked pointedly at Grace, who came in with the ladies. She crossed the room and tugged Evelyn to her feet. She and Evelyn remained standing while the women took their seats. Jennifer Sutherland passed them solemnly, without acknowledging the blunder with even a wink or smile, sympathetic or otherwise. Jennifer's cool presence made Grace feel how lacking in dignity she and Evelyn were. Her cheeks were streaked red as though she'd been slapped. She bit her lips in mute unhappiness as she watched Jennifer arrange her skirts carefully on the piano stool.

Jennifer opened a sheet of music and began to labour at the keys. The women's polite attention didn't flicker once through the long composition. Mrs. Whitby's face displayed captive interest, but she was burning inside. Grace must be confused, going home and teaching her sisters manners which were not meant for their class, and now the day she'd been waiting for, the day she had thought of for months, her flawless day, had been stained by Evelyn's impropriety.

When Jennifer finished, Mrs. Whitby rose. "That was delightful. Thank you Jennifer." She turned to Grace and Evelyn. "You've all met Grace and this is Evelyn, her sister. Grace and Evelyn lost their father this year." The women turned their attention to the sisters. "The family has four girls and three weeks ago their mother gave birth to another. That makes five." Mrs. Whitby paused. She knew she had the sincere attention of the ladies, who had been pleased with Grace's lovely face and her pleasant manners. As she continued describing the hardships in the settlement, she told the story as if she personally tended the family in the heart of the miners' quarters. "Evelyn has no hearing. She cannot hear the voice of her mother, she cannot hear the lovely songs her sister sings, she cannot hear the Reverend Mr. McCullen preach." Here was the heart of her work for all the women to see, for Mrs. Sutherland, the owner's wife, to carry with her to Halifax. Even though she was exiled in this vulgar place, she took comfort in the thought that she would be discussed in city drawing rooms.

"Evelyn is alone; she is isolated; an outcast in a closed world."

As the hostess continued to describe the family plight and retell how she had discovered Grace, ragged and uneducated, and was grooming her for better opportunities, Grace felt her chest burn with humiliation. She was not the one helping the less fortunate, she was not the girl who could move in circles outside of the mine world; she was a miner's daughter, poor and ignorant as the rest.

"And now Grace, would you sing, please." Grace heard the hostess speak as though she were far away. The women braced themselves to listen with extra attention since the poor girl was so disadvantaged.

Jennifer Sutherland struck the keys and Grace began singing. Evelyn watched the strings thrumming under the open cover of the piano. They trembled like Grace's throat did when she sang. Evelyn knew speech was connected to these tremblings. She remembered sitting on her father's lap with her head on his chest. Whenever he spoke, his chest vibrated; if he laughed it shook and rumbled. When she pushed with her stomach and huffed air out of her throat, she too felt the vibrations in her throat. And others looked at her. She was making noise when she did this. And now something was coming out of this piece of furniture. What was it?

Evelyn stepped away from Grace, who was now lost in her song, eyes closed, hands relaxed at her side, and in two steps she was beside the piano. She reached her hand inside and her fingers tapped and pulled the strings. Jennifer stopped playing. Grace stopped singing, mid-word, her eyes wide. A deep flush travelled up her neck and across her face. Unaware, Evelyn remained bent under the hood of the piano, popping the strings within her reach and making tuneless plunks.

Grace pulled her away and held her hand as the two girls stood facing the terrible quiet in the room. "Thank you, Grace," Mrs. Whitby's face was set like shock-white porcelain. She had taken Grace under her wing, but perhaps she had gone too far in her efforts of good will, perhaps it was time to distance herself from the girl. She rose. "I think that's all we have time for today. There's a basket of mending in the hallway which you can take home with you for Evelyn. Thank you for coming."

The dismissal was polite but cold. The glass

doors clicked quietly behind Grace, and she left the stately home knowing that her relationship with her gracious patron would never be the same.

CHAPTER FIVE

HANNAH LAY BESIDE GRACE, WATCHING her sleep. Yesterday when she had come back from the tea she hadn't been full of her usual annoying mannerisms, and Evelyn too had been subdued. What had happened? She wouldn't find out from Evelyn. Maybe Grace would say something. Hannah rose and stepped over her sisters to go into the next room and stir the fire. A current of wind around her ankles reminded her they would have to get some rags to push around the door.

Hannah sprinkled a hard end of bread with water to soften it. She cut it in slices and toasted it on the stove. Then she went in and roused her sisters. There was a late harvest at a farm a few miles away, and they would have to leave early if they wanted to be hired for the day. Gregory's mother would look in on their mother while they were gone.

They set out as the mist was rising off the ground and the sky was growing pale. After walking an hour they came to a farm where they lined up with other harvesters waiting to be given sacks and sent out across the fields to pull up turnips. The farmer, a thick-chested man with tense shoulders and fiery red skin, went down the line, dropping sacks at everyone's feet. Hannah and Grace led the way across the field. Theresa and Evelyn trailed behind to balance on rocks and stare at other children.

The earth was dry and caked around the bulbous turnips, and their backs soon ached from stooping and digging them out. When their sacks were filled, Hannah and Grace carried them across the fields, their backs bent double under the weight. Hannah was surprised that Grace didn't utter a word of complaint. She worked in silence, keeping up with Hannah, though her eyes were red with tears and she wiped them so often that they soon became streaked with mud. As the day passed and they moved deeper into the fields, the walk became longer and the work harder. By late afternoon, Theresa was too tired to pick any more. She jerked at the turnips, ripping off the tops. The farmer, who worked close-by, stood up and watched her. Hannah pulled Theresa's hand away and dug her fingers hard into the soil to dig out the turnip that was stuck. "Pull them gently, T'resa. Else we'll lose pay."

"I don't want to," she complained.

For the rest of the day, the farmer kept a close watch on the girls. As the sun lowered and the fields turned a dark choppy blue, the harvesters gathered the last turnips and walked to the farmhouse.

The farmer sat at a table on his porch where they gathered to receive their pay. The girls approached the table in a line. Hannah was first. Behind her, Grace carried Theresa, who nodded to sleep on her shoulder. "Coin or turnip?" the farmer asked.

"Coin," said Hannah.

The farmer placed a farthing on the table. She accepted it and moved on. Grace approached the table. The farmer called, "Next."

"Coin," said Grace.

"Move along. You've been paid already."

"I haven't."

"Your kin's got it."

Hannah moved back to the table. "What, this?"

She held out the coin. "This for all of us?"

"The two young 'uns made a mess of the fields, tearin' at the tops."

"They picked as well as any of 'em," Hannah pointed behind her to the children waiting with their families.

"They didn't carry in. I pay by the sack brought in."

"I brought in sacks and you haven't paid me," Grace said.

"That's all you're gettin'." The farmer clamped his mouth shut and the redness in his skin darkened.

The harvesters moved forward, sensing trouble with the pay. The farmer's wife interjected. "Go on now. You've been paid for your work."

"We have not! We've not been paid fairly," Grace insisted.

"You want to take money away from the others?" The farmer stood up, yelling for all to hear.

"We want what's owed us," Hannah answered in a voice as big as his.

"Get away. We'll not pay you extra!" The farmer's wife flapped her arms at them. "You're little thieves you are, just pushin' t' get what y' can with no concern for what y're takin' from the others. Robbin' out o' the mouths of everyone else. That's the problem with hirin' vagabonds."

"I deserve to be paid!" Grace cried.

"Aye, aye," said a voice in the crowd behind her. If one of them wasn't being paid fairly, it could happen to all of them.

The woman ran her eye over the sisters, measuring how much trouble they could be. She picked up a half empty sack of turnips and thrust it at Grace. "Take it an' get out of my sight."

"That's me an' Grace. What about Evelyn and T'resa?" Hannah asked.

"I'll give 'em a boot, that's what about 'em, if y' don't clear away." The farmer took a step towards Hannah. She held her ground, and he hesitated. He could pick her up and throw her away easily. But then what? The harvesters were watching in grim silence, and he didn't have his shot gun at hand. "You cheeky little maggot," he growled under his breath.

"I'll take coin for Evelyn an' Theresa."

"You'll take what I give y'," snapped the farmer's wife, wanting only to get rid of the troublesome girls before the others thought they could ask for more than they deserved. "Come with me."

Hannah hesitated a moment, then motioned to her sisters to follow. As they passed the field workers, a quiet voice said, "Good on y', girl."

The woman led them to a barn set back from the house. A few thin hens scattered as she opened the door and pointed to a heap of straw, rags and sticks. "Y' can take from there, but mind only for the two young 'uns. You two 've already been paid."

Grace lifted a tin washbasin with a jagged hole in the bottom. "This is all rubbish!"

"That what their work's worth," sniffed the woman before she left.

Hannah stepped over two broken chairs and sorted through the soiled rags. "Fetch me the sack. We can use these."

Evelyn sat on a heap of straw, too tired to stand. Theresa lay at her feet and fell asleep. Hannah grabbed handfuls of garbage and flung them aside, searching for something special, maybe a spoon or knife. Evelyn watched Hannah and idly scooped through a pile of straw by her side. Her hand struck an object, and an odd sound erupted from under a thin layer of straw.

Hannah pointed. "What was that, Ev'lyn?"

Evelyn cleared more straw away and discovered a fiddle, its wooden top blistered and swollen. She ran her fingers across the strings and broken tuners.

"She's not goin' t' let us have it," Hannah said, noticing her sister's excitement. Evelyn plucked the strings and held the fiddle to her cheek. She could feel the wood vibrate. Hannah knelt in front of her and shook her head. She reached out to take the fiddle away, but Evelyn hunched over it.

"Let her take it," Grace flopped down, unable to stand any longer. "Maybe Robbie can fix it."

"How'll we hide it?" Hannah asked.

"Put it in the sack."

Hannah picked up a strip of cloth to wrap the fiddle in, but Evelyn refused to give it up. "Y' can't carry it out, Evelyn. Come on," Hannah tugged impatiently. "I'll get it out for you." She looked at the barn door and motioned with her hands at the sack. "Hurry, she'll be back."

Evelyn clamped the fiddle tighter against her chest. Hannah yanked it roughly away from her and shoved it in the sack. Evelyn cried, a terrible, unhappy cry, with bouts of silence followed by hoarse noises that sailed out of her throat.

The farmer's wife returned to the barn. "What's wrong with her?" she asked suspiciously.

"She wants to go home," said Grace picking up Theresa, who was still asleep.

The farmer's wife looked at the pile of garbage. "What'd y' take?" She motioned to the sack on Hannah's back.

"A bit of rubbish from the pile," Hannah bolstered the sack on her shoulders.

"Let's have a look."

Hannah turned around silently so the woman could look inside. The woman pulled at the rags on the top. "Y've taken too many."

"I told y' Hannah, she'd want that spoiled snip of blue satin back," Grace used a tone of voice she'd learned at Mrs. Whitby's house, a tone which said the article was of no importance, except to someone who was too needy to pass it by.

The woman's back stiffened. She examined the scrap of blue satin and found it in such poor condition that she stuffed it back in the sack, "That's just one of my old dresses. Y' can keep that prize an' thank me in your prayers." She stepped aside to let the girls pass.

Night closed around them as they set out for home. Hannah carried the sack of turnips and rags which hid the fiddle, and Grace trudged beside her with Theresa asleep on her back. Hannah kept her head bent to the ground and watched their feet march as though a drum were keeping rhythm. It occurred to her that her sister wasn't as different from her as she had thought. She smiled at their feet trudging so well in time and felt close to Grace. Perhaps she could depend on her after all.

CHAPTER SIX

S UN STREAMED INTO THE WOOD SHOP, striking the unfinished church pews that Robbie was working on. He stepped out from behind a work bench and gave Evelyn's cheek a twist. She darted away, and he shadowed her.

"Leave off the child's play, Ev'lyn." Hannah stepped into the shop, carrying a sack.

"Leave off the child's play? Didn't think I'd be hearin' that from you," Robbie teased.

Hannah smiled and shrugged her shoulders. "Look what we got here," she said pulling the fiddle out of the sack.

Robbie turned it over and examined it on all sides. He pressed down on the top where the wood had swollen, gently testing the strength of the braces inside the body. Hannah and Evelyn watched him peer along the length of the neck to see how straight it was.

"Can it be fixed?"

"Think so. Let me hold onto it." He put the fiddle down and Evelyn picked it up.

"She's dyin' to have it." Hannah said, trusting Robbie to understand. Anyone else would have made them feel like fools, but he knew that Evelyn would play with it even if she didn't hear a note the fiddle made.

Robbie gently loosened Evelyn's grip on the fiddle. "Leave it to me love, I'll get it playin' soon enough." He spoke to her the way the family did, as if she had hearing. "Been t' see Gregory yet?" he asked Hannah.

"No, why?"

"His cousin came by for some splints, for his leg, I think." Robbie added, "He's not too badly off from what I hear."

"What happened?"

"Accident in the mine."

Hannah didn't wait to hear another word. She raced out of the shop and down the road, rocks and dirt flying off her feet. She rounded a bend towards a line of shacks where Gregory lived and stopped when she caught sight of John. The two faced each other stiffly across the road like two forms on a chess board.

"Come t' see what y've done?" John asked.

"What happened?" asked Hannah.

"What d'y think?"

"Is he bad?"

"He'll be laid up for weeks, maybe months. Just don't go passin' it off as a funny coincidence."

"So it's my fault?"

"Aye, it is," said John as he turned and walked away. "Y' shouldn't 've been where y' don't belong."

Hannah stepped inside Gregory's home. The shanties were all the same, dark and small, some more furnished, some less. The Grahams didn't have a table yet. They had just finished eating around an iron pot set on the floor.

"He's in there," Gregory's mother nodded her head towards the bedroom. "But he's tired, don't stay long."

Hannah entered the room where Gregory lay on a straw pallet on the floor. "How are y'?" she asked, kneeling beside him.

His face was pale. "Stupid thing I did. Can't not pay attention in a mine. That's what Dad kept sayin' when they were bringin' me out."

"What happened?"

Gregory shifted. "I was pickin' at a seam. My arms were tired and...."

"Pickin' at a seam? You're a breaker boy."

"Well I was pickin' yesterday, in a chamber, an' I got tired and forgot where I was. I stepped back as a cart was passin'." He closed his eyes and Hannah waited. "My pick was dangling an', I don't know how, it grabbed in the spokes and flipped out of my hands. I leapt to catch it and slipped an' before I knew it I was under the wheels...."

"You, working the walls?"

"Aye. It's only my leg though. Could've been my gut, Mr. McCullen said."

"Why were y' workin' the walls?" Hannah persisted. "Why would they have y' do that?"

Gregory shifted again and grimaced, his face whitening with pain.

"Why?"

"They just did."

"Think y' were cursed because I went down in your place?"

"No, I never did believe that. I was just tryin' t'

keep you out of the mines when I said it, because it's such a terrible place. I thought the work'd beat y' down," Gregory paused and closed his eyes. "The thing is, you're probably more suited to it than I am."

"Why'd they move you then?"

"Cause I was ready. I was working better...." Gregory didn't finish.

The puzzlement on Hannah's face suddenly cleared. She sat back on her heels, "And it was me." A surge of tears spilled down her cheeks.

"Shush. You'll make me feel worse."

Hannah wiped her eyes and stood to leave.

"Come visit," Gregory called after her as she hurried out.

EVELYN HAD ABANDONED her doll to Theresa, who was in her glory taking care of it. She had pulled most of its hair out in her efforts to comb it smooth, and its clothes were misshapen and grey from being washed in puddles and dragged through fields.

Evelyn sat at the table and fingered the strings of

the fiddle which Robbie had repaired. She held the instrument to her cheek and to her ear, she put her mouth to the *f*-holes and whooshed air through the body, she lifted the strings and let them slap down against the fingerboard so that they warbled tunelessly.

By the end the week, Grace was tired of the noise Evelyn made with her fiddle. She rapped on the table. "Evelyn stop it."

Evelyn ignored her and pulled at the strings. Grace threw the turnips she was peeling into a pot and walked around to where Evelyn sat. "Look, do it proper." She yanked Evelyn's chin up. "Do it proper!" Her grip on Evelyn's hand was tight. Rage suddenly filled her, an unexpected rage that came from nowhere and rushed at her like wind coming around a cliff. She jabbed at the fiddle, pulling at the thickest string. "That's low. Y' see. That's a low note." She wrenched Evelyn's hand up to her throat and forced out a high note. Her voice was constricted and the note sounded like a scream. Her fingers snapped the thinnest string. "That's a high note. That's high!" Evelyn started to cry. Grace flung her hand aside. "Just learn the blasted thing proper!"

"What's going on?" Hannah stepped in the door.

"I can't sing a note myself," Grace snapped. "She's been at it all day. She's bent the strings out of tune."

"It's like a dyin' dog," offered Theresa from under the table.

"I hate it. I hate it so much, I'm goin' to throw it away!" Grace shouted.

Hannah wondered if Grace had already tried. Their clothes were disheveled as if they'd been scuffling. She tapped lightly on the fiddle and motioned Evelyn to put it away. "It's late, Ev." Evelyn shook her head.

"See! She's stubborn as...." Grace tried to think of something really horrible to compare Evelyn with. A quiet tap on the door interrupted her thoughts. "Come in," she snapped.

John opened the door and stepped in.

"What do you want?" Hannah demanded.

He held out a letter. "This came a week ago. It's been at the store." John had seen the unclaimed letter resting on a ledge, like an announcement that the family had lost their credit.

Hannah snatched the letter and opened it hastily. Inside was a single sheet of paper covered with fine writing.

Grace looked over her shoulder. "Can y' read it?"

Hannah shook her head.

"Wait," Grace called after John as he walked back out. "Ask your aunt if we can bring the letter round to Gregory."

John nodded tersely. He hated this family, hated their misery and, even more, hated knowing that there was little hope left for them now. Winter was coming. With no credit from the store, no work, no money, and a sick mother, they were in trouble. Then there was Hannah. She made him furious, acting as if there were no rules for her, as if she could hold them back from the hole they were about to fall down. He would make sure he wasn't around to evict them when the time came.

CHAPTER SEVEN

"You awake, Grace?" Hannah climbed over her sister and went to the stove to stir up the ashes and get heat in the shanty.

"I'll be up in a minute," said Grace, but she didn't move. She was bored at home, and lonely. More lonely than she had ever been. Everyone had something that was important to them. Theresa had the doll, Evelyn had the fiddle, Hannah had herself – she didn't need anything else – but Grace had nothing. Since the tea she hadn't been invited back to Mrs. Whitby's and she missed her. She had nothing now except the hand mirror, and when she looked at her reflection, she saw a blank, unhappy face. Grace remembered the letter from her aunt. At least that was something to get up for. She rose and pulled on her dress.

"Grace?" Her mother whispered through dry lips.

Grace bent over her mother. "D'you want some water, ma?"

"Sit me up."

Grace helped her sit up and lean against the wall. "How're y' feelin'?"

"Better."

Grace smiled, relief flooding through her. They would be able to leave once her mother was strong enough to travel.

"What're y' smilin' like that for?"

"I don't know."

"Thought I was goin' t' leave y'?"

Grace shook her head no, but her eyes filled with tears that told the truth of her fears.

Her mother looked at her sharply. "Never mind. Make me a hot tea. Is there tea left?" Grace shook her head. "I'll have some raspberries leaves then. Good an' hot, mind." Her mother stopped her from leaving with a grip that was surprisingly strong. "The baby?"

"Elsie Fraser's got her. She's nursing her beside her own newborn. Elsie says she's fussy."

"That's all right, the fussy ones get what they need." Her mother loosened her grip on Grace's arm and sank back against the wall, closing her eyes.

Hannah had revived the fire and she and Grace huddled over the weak heat that came through the black iron plates. They heard a soft plucking in a corner behind them. It was Evelyn, lightly touching the strings of her fiddle. They watched her. She was playing quietly; she knew the difference between loud and quiet. Surprised, Hannah and Grace looked at each other and smiled.

After a breakfast of potatoes and raspberry leaf tea, the four sisters set out for Gregory's with the letter. Mr. McCullen, the minister, usually read the mail, but he was making his last visits to families homesteading in the wilderness before the winter made traveling impossible.

"I can't read every word of it," apologized Gregory when he saw the handwriting. They were crowded around his pallet, Hannah and her sisters as well as Gregory's three brothers, his parents, and John and his younger brother. He began:

Dearest Maggie,
I hope you are well enough to receive this letter. A month has passed since my visit and I honestly don't know how you are managing. Perhaps you have the help and goodwill of the community. I

*wonder if you have bought your fares to Halifax
yet. In...anti...*

Gregory stopped reading and mouthed the word silently. "I can't make this one out."

"Go on then," urged Grace.

*In....of this, I am.... dil-i -gen- tly...diligently saving
what I can so that you will have something to tide
you over at the beginning of your stay. I look forward to having you all nearby soon. (You'll be
happy to know that I've arranged for the girls to go
to a school nearby.) Love to you all and care espe-
cially well for yourself.*

Your loving sister, Catherine

When Gregory finished the letter, conversation filled the room. "Schools," said Gregory's mother. "Just like back home. I don't know why we left." She missed Scotland and often said she would go back even if it were to be in jail.

"Not where we lived," Gregory's father remind-ed her grimly.

"I can't wait," Grace said brightly.

"Y' have t' be careful in a port like Halifax," warned Gregory's father. "There's all types coming in off the boats." He suspected that the company wouldn't throw the widow and her daughters out in the cold so easily. Their father was still remembered as a fair man, and he believed they would be better off here until their mother recuperated.

"But it's true, Halifax is a much finer place and there's work there," countered Gregory's mother, who held the opposite opinion to her husband on every topic of conversation. "And work for Gregory there'd be too. Gregory's not a miner. He's gifted in other ways."

"There's money to be made here," Gregory's father said tersely.

"The sad truth is a family can't survive here without a man attached to it," Gregory's mother addressed Grace as if she was the only person with hearing in the room.

"There's talk of havin' the women an' girls do the sortin' in the yard." Gregory's father pointed out, "An' there'll be a new shaft sunk."

"Any changes can't come fast enough. That's why we have t' leave," Grace addressed Mrs.

Graham, who nodded in agreement.

"They're startin' to lay rail lines that'll come right to the mouth of the tunnel." Mr. Graham was not going to let his wife have the last word. "And a safety inspector'll be visitin'."

"Rumours an' dreams." Mrs. Graham dismissed him. "The girls'll fare much better in Halifax."

"We don't have our fares," Hannah pointed out. "They went for the last rent, an' I don't know what we'll do for this turn." She glanced at John, though she hadn't intended to.

John looked away. He hated collecting for the manager's office. The few families that didn't have credit were the ones with miners too sick to work. It was like taking food from the weak and helpless. John had been sent to do the rounds only because the Mackays had gone to Pictou harbour expecting to meet an uncle there. His ship hadn't arrived and they'd come back drunk and annoyed that they'd missed their turn at collecting.

"Cheer up, Hannah. Something'll turn up," Gregory said, and everyone agreed, though they all secretly feared it would be unlikely.

"Stay and eat with us," Gregory's mother offered. "The soup's almost done."

JOHN STOOD OUTSIDE, watching their shanty, shoulders hunched against the wind. He kept walking away and coming back. He believed it wasn't right to force people to leave their homes. His family had been driven off their farm when their crop had failed two years in a row. But it wasn't right either that a girl should go down in the mine. And why couldn't a girl go down if she had proven she could do the work?

But what if she couldn't handle it? What if she lost her head and took fright and ran through gas with a lit lamp? They'd all be blown up.

But then, Hannah would stand firm if anything happened. He could count on that.

John paced back and forth.

The family should just leave. But they couldn't because their fares had gone to pay the back rent. And their mother was sick. He knew what happened when sick parents travelled. Still, it was impossible to let a girl work underground with all of the men. He walked away again.

Terrible things happened when sick parents travelled. He thought of his parents' burial at sea. He felt his brother weep on his shoulder and remembered the salt spray in his face as he cried. The memory brought him to Hannah's door.

Hannah had been watching him through the window. She flung the door open as he approached and stood on the step without saying a word.

John returned her stare.

"What's the matter?" she asked.

"I need to talk to you."

Hannah grabbed her scarf and stepped outside. She led John away from the miners' shacks and up the hill. Once they were in the shadow of the trees she turned to him. "What is it?"

John took a deep breath. "I'm not goin' t' stand in your way of earning your family's keep."

Hannah's laugh was harsh. "So?"

It was going to be hard to carry through with this, John thought. "What I mean is, I'll not stop y' from goin' in the mine again." Hannah didn't answer. "Did y' hear?"

"It's too late," she said, watching him closely.

"Gregory's not there to change places with."

John knew how he could get her in, but he'd leave it up to her. She could figure it out for herself if she really needed to. This was all he'd come to say and it was time for him to leave. Still, he said, "I can get you in."

"What?"

"I know how."

Hannah was suspicious. "Why?"

John shrugged his shoulders. "Y' don't want to? Fine."

"Aye, I do," Hannah answered quickly.

"I'll get y' in an' then I'll have nothing t' do with you. Don't expect me t' hold your hand."

"Keep as far away from me as y' like." Excitement suddenly exploded in her chest. "You're sure?"

"I said I would," John snapped. "But y' can't be a hot-head. Y' can't stick your nose in it if you see trouble, y' can't do anything that'll make you stand out –"

"Don't worry," Hannah was annoyed. "I'll take care of myself."

"It's not you I'm worried about."

"I know about the gases, I know about the cave-ins, I know about the floods," Hannah shuddered. Her father had drowned when an underground reservoir had burst through a wall and filled a chamber.

"You've got t' choose a name. Not your father's nor any name that's connected with your family."

"Brian," Hannah said the first name that came to her mind.

John nodded. "Good."

They made plans and agreed to meet the next morning and Hannah went home. She found Grace alone at the table. Evelyn and Theresa were asleep.

"Where've you been?"

"I've got myself work!"

"Work? At this hour?"

"Yes. If you help me, then we'll be able to pay for rent and buy our fares t' Halifax."

Grace sat up, excited. "What do y' need me to do?"

"I need you t' let me do this job."

The happiness in Grace's face dimmed. "What kind of work is it?"

"First promise."

"No."

"We'll have money t' buy medicine for Ma an'

maybe half a bag of sugar."

"All right, all right."

"I'm goin' in the mine."

Grace was so shocked that she didn't say anything.

"Did y' hear?"

"I heard."

"I've already been down. Y' can't tell me I can't do it."

"Liar!"

"I have. When I was gone the day before Gregory broke his leg. I went in his place – the whole day and nobody knew. Almost nobody."

Grace's eyes widened. "What happened?"

"John caught me, but he kept his mouth shut. Now he's goin' to help."

"But you're not allowed!"

"If I'd been born a boy, I'd 've been working there two years already. So'd you." Hannah stood up impatiently. "Anyway, I'm goin' t' do it no matter what, with your help or without."

"Then do it without." Grace picked up the lantern. The light flared on the wall and slipped around the doorway as she walked away and left Hannah in the dark, feeling suddenly unsure.

CHAPTER EIGHT

"THERE'S A LAD OUTSIDE THE GATES LOOKIN' for work," John said as he collected his lantern and pick.

"Take 'im to the supervisor." George continued marking numbers in his ledger without looking up.

John went out to the gate. "Follow me." Under his breath he added, "Remember, y' only have t' say your name an' he'll tell y' t' go get your tools."

Hannah entered the mine yard, not as Gregory, a person she had imitated with difficulty, but as the boy she would have been. She'd seen him in her mind, she knew how his shoulders sloped, how his hands grasped his tools, how he walked. She stretched her legs in long strides and swung her upper body in a loping rhythm. John was surprised by her gait, which seemed entirely natural for a boy turning the corner of adolescence. He knocked at the door of the supervisor's shed and entered when he heard the supervisor shout.

"This lad here – what's your name again?"

"Brian."

"This lad here, Brian, is lookin' for work."

"What's your family name boy?" The supervisor didn't look up from the drawings on his desk.

"Scott," Hannah said the syllable in a quick low voice.

"There's no Scott family in camp. Where y' from?"

"From a ways off."

A muscle flinched in the supervisor's cheek as he scanned the plans. "Where?" He snapped.

"From over the ridge. We're homesteaders, doin' some farmin'–"

"A farm boy!" The supervisor fixed his watery eyes on Hannah. "We don't get farm boys in the mines."

"My stepfather sent me out."

"Y' go back an' tell your stepfather that we don't take on farm boys."

The supervisor put on his coat and made ready to go out to the yard. Hannah waited.

"Well that's it boy, go on!"

"I'm a strong worker. Used t' breakin' the ground for new fields."

"I've got a hill full of strong boys. And what's more, they'll be in the mines 'til they die, whereas you'll leave once the harvest's ready to be picked."

"But...but, I heard y' just lost a boy in an accident."

"How'd y' hear that?" The supervisor stopped and assessed the youth. Something different about him. Had some nerve, standing there after he'd been dismissed.

"Someone passing told us. That's what gave my stepfather the idea t' send me. I could take the lad's place 'til he's healed an' if y' like I'll stay on. He's got no use for me."

"How old are y'?"

"Thirteen." Hannah was relieved that at least she could tell the truth about her age. One less story to remember.

The supervisor hesitated. "Get your pick an' shovel. We'll try y' for a week. John'll tell y' about the fire rules. You'll work the west wall with him."

John led the way. All of the men had already gone in, and they walked alone through the tunnel, their voices echoing in the dark. John shook his head. "He's makin' it hard for y'."

"What's at the west wall?" Hannah asked as she watched the timbered roof of the tunnel.

"It's the only place in the mine where we work along a wall instead of in chambers."

Hannah nodded. She remembered the rooms she been in with their black pillars of coal which had been left to support the ceiling. Her father used to complain that the company let the miners take too much from around the pillars, leaving them barely thick enough to support the roof.

John turned off the main tunnel and led her to a smaller one on the right. He continued. "The seam's a bit messed up on the wall. It's clear an' wide in parts, but then gets broken up an' hard t' get at. The whole band's got a couple of feet of soft soil at the top that crumbles when it's worked. Y've got t' be careful y' don't get buried."

The tunnel sloped steeply and closed in around them. The air grew warm and heavy with coal dust. John ducked his head every few feet to avoid the timbers overhead. Hannah kept her pick and shovel close to her side, but they slipped through her wet palms and kept scraping and banging against the ground. As she followed John, she didn't know that the tunnel was curving westward and that they were travelling under the hills where she played, she only knew that they were walking deep into the earth, to a place where hidden water pressed against the walls, black and heavy as earth.

Her throat tightened and sweat dampened her shirt. Hannah had prepared herself for pain and hard work, but not for this sudden fear. She hadn't expected it. Her father had never talked about it, none of the men did. Fear was something they carried around silently. John stopped and turned around and Hannah realized that she was gasping and wheezing. "I...I'm all right."

"Get a hold of yourself. We're almost at the section they're workin'. If they hear y' pantin' with fear, it'll be over. They'll not trust y' to keep your head."

"Can we stop a minute?" Hannah could only see the dim globe of light in John's hand and his rumpled pants, and beyond that, nothing. Black air, black floor and ceiling floated around her, and she felt she was drowning in space.

John watched her struggle to get her panic under control. He couldn't think of anything to say.

"Sun's probably coming up." He'd grown up working outdoors in the fields and it had been hard for him too the first days underground. The worst thing was the way the day disappeared and even the seasons vanished in the miners' calendar of artificial light.

Before he could say anything else, the rumble of a coal tub and the light of a lantern filled the tunnel. John pulled her by the elbow and they stepped into a shallow space cut out of the side of the wall to let a young man pass, leading a pony harnessed to a bin of coal. The pony's muscles flexed in its light brown flanks as it walked past, leaving a familiar smell behind. Hannah could hear it snorting and straining up the tunnel and it was strangely reassuring. This was something from a world she knew, and if it existed down here, then so could she.

They continued walking down to the west wall. They passed a loop where the horses turned around and came to clusters of men picking along the wall. John stopped. "We'll start here. I'll break up. You shovel. Bin number twenty-six is ours. We get paid by how much we bring out. When it's full, call Jake, the one that passed us coming in, or Ed

– they'll hook it up t' the horses an' pull it out."

John swung his pick through the air. The blow shuddered in his chest as he made contact with the wall, breaking coal apart from rock. Hannah fell to work beside him, scraping the debris away from his feet with her shovel, leaving him clear to swing and strike again. They worked quickly together. Hannah counted time by the binful of coal rather than by the sun and the shadows on the ground. As the day wore on, coal dust filtered through her clothes and under her cap and settled in a black patch around her nose and mouth. By the time the call came to quit, Hannah's hands were blistered and her shoulders and arms were shaking. She collected her tools and moved uphill with the men, remembering to keep her head down and her gait long and loose.

Cold air streamed into the main tunnel. The miners came together at the opening and the lights of many lanterns made the walls glossy grey. Out in the yard, Hannah was disappointed to discover it was a starless night, almost as black as the mine. She walked out the gate without saying good-bye to John. Better for the men to think they'd been put together for work, but otherwise had nothing to do with each other.

Hannah slipped into the hills. Even on a clouded night she could find her way easily. She stopped at a thicket where she had hidden her tunic, and rolled back and forth on the ground to get the loosest layer of dust off, then pulled her tunic on over her pants and shirt and tied a strip of rag around her head.

Slipping lightly down the grassy slopes towards home, Hannah could see the metal hulls of wash-basins outside, faintly lighted by the night sky. Soon winter would send the men washing indoors. She stayed in the shadows and stepped on to her porch, looking for the washbasin, but discovered it was gone. Not only was Grace not with her, she was going to be against her. Hannah opened the back door.

The room was warm and smelled of turnips. Her place was set at the table and by the stove was the washbasin, half filled with heated water. The room grew quiet as Hannah surveyed the comforts her sisters had prepared for her and as her sisters looked over Hannah's blackened face and hands and the trembling of her tired body.

"Come get yourself washed. This pot'll fill it up," Grace said fighting a sudden urge to cry. She was frightened to see Hannah as a miner and she wanted her changed back to normal.

"I'll do your back, Hannah," Theresa offered, clutching the rag and soap so that no one else should take the opportunity away from her. Hannah dropped her tunic to the ground. "Oh, you look like a boy," she gasped.

"Hannah?" A weak call came from their mother in the other room.

Grace went to the doorway quickly. "She's just in the bath, Ma."

"I need a walk around."

"I already gave you one today. Sure y' don't....?" Grace saw her mother's head nod down on the straw. She turned back to Hannah and her sisters who were frozen in their places. "She's in an' out of sleep between one word an' the next. Hurry up, Hannah, and get cleaned up. One day she'll surprise us and walk into the room herself."

CHAPTER NINE

IT WAS SATURDAY NIGHT. THE FIRST TWO WEEKS in the mines were over and Hannah had become a miner. There'd been no time for fear after the first moment, no time for hesitation. She'd had to throw herself into the work and think on her feet, even for simple things, things she'd never considered, like what to do when she had to pee. The boys just wandered over to a wall and undid a few buttons. Hannah had to make sure she was the last one in the tunnel at break time before she could relieve herself. It was a nuisance, because John tended to match his pace to hers until one day she'd snapped at him to go ahead. He'd looked at her with confusion, then noticed her legs jiggling on the spot and registered her need with a loud, embarrassed, "Aye! I'm off."

Hannah had become a miner in every way. The

fog of coal dust she worked in everyday no longer choked her; her muscles grew stronger and her palms thickened. She developed a sixth sense that opened up the darkness and made it full of subtleties; she kept a watchful eye on the lamps and felt the air currents, the rumble of carts, the clod of ponies; she knew when to stand clear and when to throw herself into the work, and the men accepted her as one of their own, as a mate who shared the burden and the danger.

Hannah sank into the washbasin. She scrubbed herself well on Saturday night to clear away all traces of the mine and prepare for Sunday when she went outside, her skin marbled only with the blue of her veins, her hair free of the dust that cast over the miners.

"They were makin' a bad noise today," Theresa informed Hannah while she scrubbed her back.

"Doin' what?"

"Just makin' noise."

"Music," Grace corrected her. She and Evelyn had spent the afternoon trying to work out the notes to a song. Evelyn was slowly learning to understand that when Grace put her hand high in the air, she meant her to pluck the fiddle's thin strings, and when she lowered her hand, she wanted her to touch the thicker strings. Grace moved her hand up and down an imaginary scale and tapped out the rhythm of the song on the table. When she and Evelyn worked on their music they didn't feel time pass, they didn't hear the sour noises the fiddle made; they were captivated by each small step they took together.

On Sunday Robbie came to their shanty, afraid he'd find the family in a wretched state. Hannah hadn't come to his shop in two weeks and her absence worried him. "Where've y' been, girl? I've been worried."

"Workin'."

"Whereabouts?"

"A ways off. I don't get back 'til after dark, what with the walk an' all."

"By yourself?"

"Don't worry, I take the hills."

Robbie shook his head. "Winter's comin'. If y' fall down an' strike your head, well, you'll lie there, an' by the time someone sets out lookin' for you...." He left the thought unfinished. What could he do for her anyway? He worked too late to go out and meet her on the road, pressed as he was to finished the church by Christmas.

"It's only for a short time," Grace said. "Ma's getting better. She sits up every morning."

"And it's not even snowin' yet," Hannah pointed out.

Robbie held his tongue, but he was watchful. It was unusual for Grace and Hannah to be in such agreement.

"Robbie, listen t' the song Ev an' I can do." Grace stood at the head of the table and motioned to Evelyn to get her fiddle. Hannah noticed that Grace had regained her old posture. Her back was straight and she held her head up. She used to think that her sister was acting high and mighty when she stood like this. Now she realized it was just Grace being happy and feeling she belonged in the world.

Grace held her hands out until Evelyn was ready with her fiddle. They watched each other and Grace began singing a simple melody while her hands directed Evelyn to the beat and high and low notes. Evelyn plucked along, and though her notes wandered off tune, she followed Grace's song. When they finished, there was a moment of silence.

Robbie let out a long whoosh of breath as

though he'd been holding it in, in case it ruffled and dispersed the tentative song. He stood up, his flat leathery fingers folding his cap into a ball, and extended his hand to Evelyn. She took it shyly. "Thank you," he whispered.

Robbie loved music. He had come over from Scotland as a piper but had found work with a carpenter, and as time went by, he played less and less. The last time he'd taken out his pipes was to bury Hannah's father, who had been his best friend. He turned to Grace, his face full of light. "Come to my shop an' I'll add my pipes to your song."

The next evening, Grace made an early dinner, left a covered bowl of soup on the table for Hannah and checked on her mother, who was sleeping soundly, before she walked up the road with Evelyn and Theresa. Robbie's shop was swept clean and his work benches were pushed to the side so there was room to sit in a circle. They looked at each other, smiling and shy for a moment.

"D'y know this one?" Grace sang part of a melody in a soft whispery voice.

"Aye," Robbie filled his bags with air. "Sing it loud."

Grace let her voice soar. She tapped the beat on her leg with one hand and slid her other hand up and down an imaginary scale which Evelyn tried to copy on the fiddle's fingerboard. They made strange music, with Evelyn's shaky notes shadowing the haunting cry of Robbie's bagpipes and Grace's lovely voice. Their music carried outside and drew the miners in to see who was playing. Some brought tambours or fiddles, some clapped their hands and stamped their feet, some sat quietly and let the music fill them with memories. Evelyn watched the fingers of a mandolin player, she felt the vibrations of the bodhráns, she watched Grace's mouth and hand signals and tried to follow the other players, plucking the strings valiantly.

As the October sleet came and the nights turned cold, the windows of Robbie's shop steamed up and shook with laughter and music.

WHEN HANNAH CAME OUT OF THE TUNNEL, she dug her hands in her pockets and hunched her shoulders against the wind. A black layer of frost crunched under her feet. She thought of the warmth in Robbie's shop and hurried out the gate, nodding to George who counted out the men and boys. If she was quick enough getting home and bathing, she would make it to Robbie's before they finished playing.

George touched his cap. Brian was one of the last ones out. He'd been at the end of the wall with John. The two of them made a good team. They'd been sent in with the more experienced miners to see what could be got out of a break in the seam. As far as George was concerned, Brian was all right. Quick, agile, minded his own business – almost too well. Some of the others had trouble with that kind of reserve. Mind you, he personally didn't. As long as the boy worked as well as he did, he could be as mute as he liked. He'd heard them planning though to take the lad out and "loosen him up." George usually turned his eye the other way, no use inviting trouble, but he sensed from the way Scotty Mackay'd been gathering up his clan that it wasn't going to be the usual lark. No, they wanted to get under the skin of this one.

George closed the gates after the last of the men. If there was to be trouble at least it wasn't going to be on company property. He locked the chain and as he turned, he caught sight of Brian scampering across the frozen hills of slag, and in the shadows he could make out a pack of men trailing the boy. He called out and the youth stopped, alert, almost too alert. Did he know he was being followed? Scotty and his clan watched from the shadows. Must be careful now, don't want to bring trouble on yourself. Anyway, what could he tell the boy that would help? Take it in good humour and they'll go easier on you? He called out, "Get yourself right home with your earnings, lad."

The boy nodded briefly, not a word wasted, and ambled off across the sparkling heaps of rubble. George put the keys in his pocket and turned towards home, thinking of his bath and his mutton stew, his job done, the company grounds secured, the cluster of predators slinking after the boy fading in his mind the way they vanished into the night.

Hannah's earnings clacked deep in her pockets. There was something special she wanted to buy. But could she spare the money? She divided the coins in her mind: oats, potatoes, salted mackerel, the rent. After everything was paid and a bit put aside for Halifax, there might be a farthing to save. Probably not, but she liked to imagine that she could, redividing the money in her mind.

Hannah stopped abruptly, aware of a scuffling behind her. In the silence she could hear muffled laughter and a cough. The men were not being careful, knowing that they were deep in the woods and near their target. They could round the lad up between them. It was good sport to have a run with a target. Scotty called it a fox hunt. The men readied themselves to spring forward, expecting the youth to hesitate, to survey the darkness, to call out. But this lad didn't do that. He bolted, and in a flash was enveloped by darkness.

"He's out of his burrow!" whooped Scotty's cousin, Eddie.

The element of surprise was turned around and it was the stalkers who were caught unprepared and clumsy as they stumbled forward, uncertain of where their prey had vanished. The figure ahead of them had dissolved into the woods as if it had been a low cloud. In the distance they could hear the rustling of the boy fleeing, but being unused to the tricks of the wind and the hills which picked up sounds and flung them in different directions, they scattered in circles.

Hannah hurled herself through branches,

through knitted brambles and upturned roots; she dropped waist deep in holes hidden by fallen leaves and flung herself up and forward, her hands clawing at stumps, pushing off rocks, her breath sharp with pain. She navigated the woods with her senses, following paths her body remembered, and eventually came out at the other side of the hill where the amber lights of the settlement shone below. Trembling and out of breath, Hannah reached under the roots of a tree where her clothes were protected from rain and snow. She picked up a crust of frost and passed it across her face. It melted into black water and scratched her skin, but she picked up another handful of frost and another until the ice melted clear and her face was chafed clean and red.

Hannah stumbled down the hill and crept home. Once safely inside, she sank down on her knees. The room was quiet. Her mother slept soundly. Why had they come after her? Did they know? Hannah got to her feet and stumbled to the stove to put water on to heat. They couldn't know, because there would be more of an uproar, but still, something was wrong. Something about her wasn't the same as the other miners, even though she had tried her best, something wasn't right.

FROST-COVERED TREES stood like mauve thistles on the hills. It was Sunday, Hannah's day off. They had spent the morning gathered with the Reverend Mr. McCullen and now the afternoon lay ahead of them to rest. Hannah sat by the window with Grace, sewing a border on a blanket for Winnie made from the rags they'd collected. Her fingers had thickened with mine work, and the needle felt fine and slick against her skin.

She looked at Evelyn, who sat by her feet. When she played at Robbie's shop her colour was high, excitement trembled in her arms, and her fingers slid and stabbed at the fingerboard. Even with the sour notes she played and the times when she'd take a path suddenly different from everyone else, her music belonged in the circle at Robbie's as much as anything else, because it was like life in the mines. It was a groping in the dark, it was faith and hope. If Evelyn had a bow, thought Hannah, her music would hang in the air, would carry like Robbie's pipes, calling out even louder than it did now.

Robbie had told her there was a fiddler who came to the settlement every few months to sell bridles and reins for horses. He was deft with his hands and might be able to make a bow for Evelyn.

"I want it soon," Hannah had told him. She only put aside a farthing, but she wanted it.

"I don't even know if he can do it," Robbie had warned. "Don't get carried away with the idea of gettin' Ev'lyn a bow."

"What if we got him everything he needed?" Hannah had insisted. "What would he need?"

"I don't know. A good dry piece of wood – I've some that's been lyin' around for a couple of years – he could take what he needed, and horse hair, I imagine."

"I can get that."

"Y' can?"

Hannah had almost said "At the mine," but she had caught herself. She knew which pony would provide the threads for the bow; a dappled grey with a tail so long it touched the ground. She had seen it flick like a spray of white water in the dark.

Hannah moved away from the window and sat beside the stove with her sewing. Had Robbie contacted the fiddler yet? Her foot jiggled restlessly. It didn't matter, she told herself. The important thing was to have everything ready for when the man came to town.

"Ma's been up walkin' a bit every day this week." Grace lit the lamp as the afternoon deepened to night. "It'll be time to stop soon."

"I know."

"Once she's up, she won't let y' work in the mine."

"She's not up yet," Hannah only half-listened to Grace. How could she get to the stables without being noticed?

"It won't be long," warned Grace.

Hannah nodded absently. How would she get it without the pony bucking and neighing? She needed a sharp knife. Hannah's needle attacked the cloth in quick jabs; she sewed without seeing what was in her hands; her mind scuttled along the walls of the stable, finding the darkest corners, the shortest path to the dappled pony. She would have to be careful. What had happened yesterday was a warning.

CHAPTER TEN

JOHN STAYED BY THE GATE AND WATCHED. The snow showed up streams of men as they left the mines. Hannah's figure was solitary, heading west away from the settlement. She would double back in the hills. John had heard the men teasing Scotty and his brothers for losing Brian in the woods and he realized how unsafe it was for her now. It would only be a few more weeks before she left. He tried to comfort himself with the thought, but instead it pricked at his chest. His kinship with Hannah had grown unexpectedly deep. Her determination fueled his own hopes and the dreams he shared with no one.

John remembered how his father used to talk about Nova Scotia as if it were a paradise. He used to say it was a place for farmers, a place where there was good land to be claimed and settled. But none of them had known the journey across the ocean would be so difficult. There was nothing to go back to Scotland for, and John swore he would never sail across the waters of the Atlantic again. He wanted to farm, wanted to stake a claim once his brother was old enough to help him break up new fields. He hoped his uncle and cousins would as well. He kept his thoughts to himself. It was a way of protecting his dreams, and he was determined not to give them up, though it happened to most of the miners who were eventually worn down with work or injury or sickness.

When he saw Hannah blend into the haze of the tree line, he turned and headed home. No one was following her.

HANNAH FELT THE MINERS WERE watching her and she knew John sensed it too. She could feel the tension in his back and his quiet long stares. There was only a short time left to work. She had almost replaced the train fares and all that she wanted in the next few days was to get the bow for Evelyn.

At the end of the day, Hannah finished her work

quickly. She pushed past John, her head down, her loping gait stretched to its fullest. She had to get to the stable. She knew that Jake would take the harnesses off the ponies and the two stable boys would brush them down outside. Hannah had been watching them, looking for a safe moment to slip in and take what she wanted. The problem was, there was no opening for her to get in, not one. She'd thought about leaving the pit during lunch, but it would be strange to see her crossing to the stables. What would her reason be for going there? If she hid and waited until the gates were closed and locked, she'd have time to get the horse hair, but what about getting out afterwards? The guard dogs would bark, and everyone would know there was an intruder at the mine. No, there was no opportunity. It meant that Hannah had to do it openly, but at the best opportunity. She chose the time when there was the most commotion in the yard: quitting time.

When John came out of the tunnel, Hannah had disappeared. He walked out the gate and looked towards the hills, but couldn't see her. She must have dashed home quickly. He left the gate.

Jake stripped the harnesses off the ponies and

the stable boys ran their brushes over their flanks with fast flicks. The feed was ready in the cleaned stalls. While the boys were busy outside, Hannah walked into the dark stables. She walked confidently, as if she belonged, and no one seemed to notice her. Two ponies were already in the stable for the night. One was the dappled grey. Hannah opened the blade of her father's pocket knife and looked at the pony's white tail cascading to the ground. A few strands would surely be enough. She patted the pony's round hindquarters and made a soft murmur. The pony looked around, chewing a mouthful of hay. She sorted through its hair and separated it into thirds as though she were going to plait it. She ran her thumb lightly across the blade of her knife and felt its sharpness. Her heart pounded. She took a deep breath, flashed a quick look at the open door and ran the blade across the hair. It cut away easily. She looked at the milky swath in her hand with disbelief. She could hear Jake talking softly to a pony as he led it into the stable. Hannah quickly stuffed the hair into her shirt and walked towards the entrance. Jake was startled when her saw her.

"What're y' doin' here?"

"Visitin' the old grey," Hannah continued on her way, but Jake stepped in her path.

"What for?"

"I saw him stumble. Thought there might be somethin' sharp in his hoof."

"It's my job t' see t' that. Why didn't y' tell me?"

Hannah shrugged. "Suppose I wanted t' see for myself."

Jake's usually gentle face hardened with anger. "After my job are y'?"

"No."

"The west wall's too hard for y', is it?"

"No, I swear!"

Jake's hand shot out to grab Hannah by the collar. She jumped back and put up her fists, ready to swing. "Stay back," she called out.

"You little scab, I'll rub your face in the ground."

Before Jake could lunge again, a snarl cut between them. "Cut it out!" The supervisor stepped into the barn and gave Hannah a cold stare. "You're out of your place. Don't let me catch y' here again."

Hannah turned and walked away. Jake's eyes burned with distrust as he watched her leave the gate. Outside, she turned west and ran for the hills, the pale night sky and fields of snow whirling in a bowl around her. She slowed down and caught her breath as she approached the shelter of the trees. She could feel the rough strands of hair under her shirt. She had everything now for the bow. Normally, Hannah would have noticed the footprints at the tree line or the tracks leading from the mine gates to her path in the woods, but she was so caught up with her prize that she didn't look around.

The attack happened fast. Hannah didn't have a chance to cry out when she was knocked to the ground and dragged by the legs though the woods. Snow slid down her neck, it filled her ears and mouth and scraped her face, and she struggled to keep her head up so it didn't choke her.

After being pulled along the ground for a while, her legs were released. Hannah tried to get to her feet, but a foot on her back held her down, face forward in the snow. She could see half a dozen pairs of blackened boots. She saw a thick rope coiled on the snow. Someone picked it up and flung it into the air. By the snap of twigs, she knew it was thrown over tree branches. Her feet were tied with one end of the rope, and with grunts and hoots, the young men hoisted Hannah up out of the snow by her feet. The rope was tied off and there she hung upside-down in the dark.

Snow trickled over her face, her pockets emptied themselves, the pony hair slid to her throat and her cap started to slip off her head. Hannah reached up and held her cap down. Instinct told her to conserve her energy and not scream or writhe on the line.

Scotty circled the rope. "Brian, my boy, it's time t' get t' know one another, see. We'd 'a liked t' do it another way, but y' never come an' share a pint with us."

Brian remained silent. His stillness irritated Scotty. It was almost as if the lad didn't care what happened to him.

"Is he a mute?" Eddie half-joked.

"He can talk when it suits him," Charlie observed.

"We'll make it suit him," said Scotty. They stood in a circle and pushed her between them. She swung around, picking up speed, making a bigger circle, round and round until the blood pounded in her head. Her cap slipped to the side as her hands loosened. Black night and silver branches swirled together around her, laughing faces passed upside-down, and rough soot-black hands grasped her shoulders and flung her faster around.

Like a spring wound too tight, Hannah suddenly exploded. A scream tore from her chest, her cap flew off and her hair uncoiled like a ball of black fire. Her hands, no longer occupied with her cap, scratched and punched as she passed around the circle. The young men fell back, some in the snow, some on their knees, quickly scrambling a safe distance away. They got to their feet, open-mouthed, and watched Hannah slow down, her circles gradually becoming smaller until she swayed back and forth.

A red welt throbbed on Scotty's cheek. "We've been deceived lads." He spat in the snow. "We've been stabbed in the back. The mines're contaminated. They might as well be closed with the plague that's in there now."

"Y' laid a plague, y' did," Eddie gasped, afraid of death choosing him as its next victim.

"That's not true," Hannah shouted.

"Shut up!" Charlie yelled.

"Give it to her, Scotty," Archie was enraged.

"Go ahead y' cowards. Kick at me while I'm

trussed up and helpless. Go ahead!"

"She's right," Scotty said with a cold smile. "Fair's fair now, lads. She does the work of a man so she should be treated like a man." They agreed with him, not sure what he meant, but confident that it wouldn't be pleasant. "Let's start with that mess of hair. That's not how a proper lad should wear his hair, is it?" Scotty took out a knife. "Let's clean that up." He stepped forward and Hannah swung at him.

"Hold her, lads."

She jerked her body on the line and shook her head back and forth but Charlie and Archie held her tightly and steadied her head for their brother. Scotty grasped a handful of hair and sliced it off with his knife. Hannah's teeth snapped the air as she tried to bite his hands. "You're a vicious little rat, you are," he cursed.

"Wait till Dad hears about this," Charlie laughed.

"The whole damn county'll hear about this," Scotty chopped a last handful of hair. "There, now y' look like a proper lad. A right ugly one."

They released her and stepped back quickly out of her reach. "You haven't got the courage to give me a fightin' chance," she gasped. "Cut me down."

"No, " Eddie warned. "She might get away."

"Like she did last time," Archie said. "This here's Hannah of the hills."

"Bring the men 'round," Charlie agreed.

"We're goin' t' have a trial," Scotty was excited. "We'll prove she's a witch. Let's go get Dad and the others." Hannah shuddered. The men in the barracks would come out, hungry for trouble. "She's tied up tight. She can't get away."

"What do they do t' witches?" Charlie asked as they turned to go.

"Give her a public floggin' t' start," Scotty's voice carried in the dark. "Then burn her."

Their voices retreated to silence. The moon cast its light on the snow and made the darkness strangely bright. Where would she be flogged? In front of the church? Before Evelyn and Theresa and Grace? Hannah imagined the crowd that would gather. The men would be calling for her blood.

"Dad?" Hannah was surprised to hear her own voice come out clear as if she were calling her father to dinner. She strained her head up to see how she was fastened to the tree. The rope around her ankles looked far away. She reached her arm up. The distance between her fingers and the knot stretched like a field. Hannah let her head fall back. The longer she stayed upside-down, the weaker she grew. She brought her head up again and heard a whisper, "Hannah, you're as sturdy as a rope."

"Dad, help me," she called out, crunching her stomach muscles and forcing her shoulders to curl around. She felt cold and alert. Hannah ran her hands over her pockets. Everything had fallen out. Her fingers brushed something smooth balanced on a shelf of material at the mouth of her pocket. It was her father's pocket knife. She froze and carefully closed her fingers around it. The wooden handle was warm. She brought it to her cheek, feeling her father's hand in the wood.

Hannah crunched her body up and tried to reach the rope, but fell back. Her head pounded with pressure. She needed momentum. She forced her shoulders back and brought her weight forward with her legs. Her arms pumped and gradually, panting and sweating, she began to swing, arching her body back and pulling her weight around and forward on the return. She reached for the rope, but still couldn't grasp it. Her thighs burned as she shortened her legs, curling forward each time in a ball. Hannah pushed harder and harder, pulling herself around with each swing, until her fingers grasped the rope, but she was moving with such force that the weight of her body swinging back broke her hold.

Exhausted, Hannah let her body swing aimlessly. "Come on Hannah, come on girl, you can do it," she heard her father say, as he had one night long ago when she'd been lost in the woods. He'd found her when night had been so thick that she couldn't see her feet and was afraid to take a step. His hand had held hers, wide and warm and prickly with coal grit, and he'd coaxed her out of the forest to the small clearing where her mother had stood waiting outside the shanty.

"I can't." Her words unfurled in white clouds from her mouth. "I can't."

"Give it one more try. That's my girl."

"I can't." Her head ached.

"Don't cry. You'll get it this time. Come on girl."

Hannah took a breath and began again. She had to pump hard to regain her momentum. She put the pocket knife between her teeth and hurled through the night with all the force she could manage, curling up so tightly she felt her muscles would rip. She grasped the rope with both hands and held fast until she stopped swinging in sharp, uneven circles. Holding on tight, she cut the thick fibers. Her legs dropped through the air like rocks, the rope slid through her fingers, and she fell to the ground.

CHAPTER ELEVEN

HANNAH CAME TO HER FEET SLOWLY. SHE saw her hair on the snow. It was unreal, like strange moss clumped around her feet. She gathered it up and crept away through hidden trails back to the settlement.

Hannah surveyed the dark rows of shacks before going down the hill. It was quiet. The stillness could be a trap, she thought, her heart pounding, her stomach sick. She slid down the slope on the back of her heels, shoulders hunched low, and crept along the shadows towards her home. She slipped inside her door and slammed it shut, barricading it with her body, her face pressed against the rough wood. The smell of her home was familiar. She knew where the table and chairs were, where the stove was, where her sisters sat, and, without looking around, she began to cry.

For a moment, Theresa, Evelyn and Grace wondered who the lad was with the bleeding ankles and ragged hair, with hands full of soot and blood.

Hannah's mother stood behind her. Grace had roused her when Hannah hadn't come home. "Oh, my girl, they've hurt you."

Hannah half-turned and fell into her mother's arms. She could hear her mother speaking, the door opening and closing, her sisters rustling silently and intently at the tasks they were given. She was undressed and bathed. Her mining clothes were tied in a tight bundle and fed to the fire in the wood stove. The floor was swept of coal dust and burrs and twigs.

"They're comin' for me, Ma," she mumbled as her mother dressed her.

"Who?"

"They want t' burn me."

"Grace, go get Robbie. And mind yourself." She turned back to Hannah. "I should've known. Your comings and goings were too familiar, but I was too weak to think of it."

The sound of shouting came towards their shanty. "Go and bed yourself down. Theresa and Evelyn, get in there too." The three girls hurried into the other room and huddled on the straw.

The door burst open and Hannah's mother stepped up to the threshold. "What's this?"

"You know why we're here, Maggie," Scotty Mackay's father looked into the room behind her. "Where's Hannah?"

"What do you want?"

"She's cursed us." He turned to the men behind him and shouted, "Disguised herself as a boy, and now every one of us'll be victim to the disasters lyin' there waiting for us. She's the one's laid trouble in the tunnels! And she's goin' t' pay!!"

"Are y' gone half mad?"

"Are y' tellin' me she wasn't in the mines?" Mackay spoke slowly.

"What would she be doing there? With all the men who've watched her grow up? Any one of them'd recognize her. Why don't you ask?" Hannah's mother called to the men behind Mackay. "Was Hannah in the mines?"

"I'm askin' you," Mackay insisted.

"Course not," Maggie scoffed.

"Then y' don't mind us comin' in an' havin' a look."

Mackay stepped forward and Maggie blocked the

door, her feet spread wide. "She's asleep." She could see the glow of lanterns illuminating the doorways across from theirs and a cluster of women and children gathered outside to watch.

When Robbie and Grace rounded the lane, they saw the pathway choked with miners.

"What's going on?" Robbie addressed the men. His query was met with silence. They themselves were not sure of the unbelievable story.

"Hannah's been workin' at the mine," Scotty said. "She disguised herself. Called herself Brian."

"Aye, kept to himself too much, so we thought we'd meet up after work an' get t' know the lad better," added Charlie.

"Not *the lad*," snapped Scotty, *"her."*

"So y' had a chat with the lad after work, an' what happened?"

"We discovered it was Hannah."

"Then where is she?"

"We had her up in the hills."

"How many of you?" Maggie's voice was sharp.

"What does it matter?" snapped Mackay.

"I'm curious to know how many young men she supposedly fought off."

"She didn't fight us off," Scotty countered, wary

of his reputation. "We had her tied up."

"The group of y' went an' tied up a young girl in the woods?! I think you're out huntin' the wrong person!" Maggie raised her voice and the men fell back, listening intently.

Scotty could feel the turn behind him. "I'm tellin' the truth. We had her upside-down in a tree and we cut her hair as proof. Go in the house an' you'll see."

"Well if y' had someone tied up by the feet in the middle of the woods why aren't y' lookin' there?"

"We been there," Eddie piped up. "She were gone. Just the rope hangin' there all alone."

"So a young girl, tied up by six lads an' left hangin' upside-down just up an' cut herself down?" Robbie almost spat out the question.

"Or she was cut down – maybe by the likes of you," Mackay pointed out, trying to turn the men back around.

"I don't think so, sir. I've been at my shop all afternoon, and there's half a dozen men who'll prove it. Which is more than I can say for your clan, getting half the village up with their stories."

"We'll see tomorrow whether this Brian shows up for work," Scotty was furious.

"He'd be a fool to go back after what y've done t' him." Maggie's sharp voice carried to the back of the crowd.

"It's her all right. We know it's her. The first time we tried t' get her, she got away, an' everyone knows that Hannah slips around these hills like an Indian," Charlie sputtered.

"Shut up," snapped Scotty.

"So this is the second time you've been after the lad? If I were him, I wouldn't show my face again. It'll mean nothing tomorrow if he's not at the mine," Robbie laughed.

Muttering, the miners dispersed and the lanterns were brought back inside. Mackay stepped close to Robbie, hatred in his eyes. "You've made a fool of my boys."

"They've made fools of themselves."

"They're tellin' the truth an' it'll come out sooner or later."

"If the truth were something that came out as surely as the sun, then you'd have been driven out of the settlement by now."

"Watch how y' speak t' me."

"Are y' threatenin me?"

"I'm just tellin y' to watch yourself."

Robbie stepped inside and closed the door. Maggie was seated at the table with Grace.

"Ma?" Hannah came into the room. Her mother's eyes were closed and her skin was strangely colourless. Hannah glanced at Robbie. He looked as if the wind had been knocked out of him. His mouth hung open and his eyes watered. Without a word, he turned and walked out. Hannah began to cry.

"It's all right, Hannah. I didn't have a chance to tell him, and you're a sight," her mother comforted her.

"I'm goin' t' run away tonight," Hannah cried, wiping her eyes, but more tears kept running down her cheeks. "I'm goin' to get away from here and I'm never comin' back."

"That's as daft as goin' in the mine in the first place," her mother snapped. Her mouth was a pale line, but her eyes glittered as she watched Hannah. "What did y' think y' were doing? Were y' thinkin' at all? Y' wouldn't 've seen the light of day again if they'd 've discovered you in the tunnels."

"The whole time she couldn't be talked out of anything she set her mind to!" Grace interjected, afraid now, and furious that Hannah had made all of this happen.

"I hold y' both responsible," their mother said sharply, then her shoulders rounded and her eyes grew watery. "Lord, I'm tired." She rubbed her face. "Too tired t' scold." She took a shaky breath. "We'll leave together. Not one of us'll be separated. That's what y' did it for, isn't it?" She looked between Grace and Hannah. They nodded. "Get on then, make me a cup of tea." She sat back. When they got up from the table, she muttered under her breath. "I must be daft, but I couldn't be prouder."

CHAPTER TWELVE

T HE STILLNESS OF HANNAH'S DAYS WAS unusual. She stayed indoors, away from the window at the back of the shanty, mostly sitting idle, noticing how the lines of soot around her nails were fading. Robbie hadn't come by. Perhaps he mistrusted her. Perhaps he'd struck her from his heart. She didn't think about it long. It worried her too much.

"I've not made y' prisoners, have I?" she asked one morning as she noticed Grace pouring the last of the porridge into a pot.

"What d'y' mean?" Grace asked.

"Not daring to go out an' buy food."

Her mother laid the bowls on the table. "I'm goin' out this very morning."

Hannah had been inside for four days. She walked around the cabin restlessly while she watched her mother pull a shawl around her head and shoulders.

"Stay back from the door now," she said to Hannah. "Grace, lock up after me."

November snows had fallen, and the air was cold and bright. Hannah saw daylight fall on the floor like a white cloth, but Grace closed the door abruptly before she could see outside. "The nerve of them, watching the door as if the king was about t' come out." Grace barricaded the door, then walked over to the stove and fidgeted with the pot and ladle. Her uneasy clatter got on Hannah's nerves.

"Stop fussin'!"

"No!"

"Then do somethin' useful." Even as Hannah said it, she knew there was nothing to do. They weren't making candles, they weren't preserving food, they weren't keeping up their supplies for the winter. They were just waiting to leave.

"I'll cut your hair," Grace said suddenly.

"Oh yes!" Theresa cried. She didn't like Hannah's hair. It frightened her.

Hannah shrugged and nodded. "Y' can't make it any worse, I s'pose."

Grace took a flat leather pouch out of a bag of their father's belongings that was kept in a corner behind the stove. She unrolled it and removed his razor. Theresa and Evelyn watched as Grace trimmed Hannah's hair. When it was finished, they stood in front of her.

"You look good," said Theresa with relief.

Grace laughed. "It does suit y'."

Hannah ran her hand though her hair. "It's fine," she said and flung her arms around Grace.

Their mother stepped in quickly through the back door.

"You're home early," Grace said. She noticed her mother's basket was empty. "What's happened?"

"Oh they're gossiping. Sayin' that as Hannah hasn't been seen for a week, it's giving the boys' story some weight. Just idle tongues." She looked around at Hannah. "That looks better, love."

"Where's the food, Ma?" Hannah asked.

"They wouldn't sell t' me. Refused my money. Said it was made at the expense of all the men in the settlement. Nonsense like that. Your father and Mackay were on opposite sides of the fence over every little thing. Now Mackay's talkin' all over town, putting us down to the lowest. Tomorrow's Saturday and the last chance t' leave before...." She left the sentence unfinished.

Before the miners' day of rest. Hannah thought. Before they'd have the day idle to come around and demand to see her.

Her mother continued, "We'll be off on the mornin' train. I'll go see Robbie this afternoon. Grace, go over to Elsie Fraser an' collect Winnie. An' give her this." She undid a silver locket from around her neck. "Tell her I'm grateful for what she did." She took a deep breath, and Hannah noticed she was shaking. "I'll have a rest before we start collecting our things."

It didn't take them long to fill a few baskets with their clothes, their bowls and spoons, their needles and iron cooking pot. They ate potatoes for supper and, since they wanted to save the oil in the lamp, they blew out the wick and lay down early. It wasn't until late at night, though, that they finally fell asleep.

They dressed in two layers for their journey, not knowing how cold it would be on the train, and wore shawls wrapped around their heads to keep the biting cold from their ears and neck. As they stood with their baskets and bundles, ready to step outside, panic beat in Hannah's chest.

Grace opened the door, and they left the safety of their shanty. The sun reflected off the snow into

Hannah's eyes. She squinted and looked down, unused to the outdoor light. Just ahead of her on the ground, she saw the tip of a wooden crutch. She looked up. Gregory smiled, and his mother, supporting him on the side where he had no crutch, smiled too. Beside them, Robbie nodded at her and held out his hand. "All set?"

Hannah took his hand, and they moved up the path, past weather-beaten shanties, past black windows pressed close with faces.

"Look at 'em gawkin'," their mother said scornfully.

Gregory and his mother hobbled behind them. "That's because the most famous person in the place is passin'," Gregory called out. He smiled at Hannah when she looked back.

"Who, me?" Theresa asked.

"Aye, you," Robbie picked her up and carried her on his hip.

Hannah was relieved to be outside. She had felt trapped inside their shanty, and it had made her afraid, so afraid that she jumped at every creak of wind coming through the walls and had strange dreams, imagining miners tunnelling underground and coming up out of the floor like black beetles, scuttling after her because she had delivered a curse on the mines. But now in the outside air, with the smell of evergreens eddying around them, she knew there was nothing wrong with her. She raised her head to meet the looks of suspicion, of curiosity, and awe that shone out of the faces of children and women as she passed.

Far in the distance, Hannah could see a thin line of smoke from the train. The small passenger platform was empty, except for a solitary miner who turned around when he heard their footsteps. It was John, his face blackened with coal dust.

"Y' shouldn't 've come," Hannah said. "They'll know y' had a part in it."

"I don't care."

"I messed up," she said sadly.

"How were y' supposed to keep away from them when they were so stuck on getting you? I'm sorry myself. I should've left it alone."

"No y' shouldn't." Hannah was unused to speaking with John. They had grown accustomed to working together – they anticipated each other's moves and understood each other's gestures, and the more they had worked together, the less they had talked. They looked at each other, tongue-tied.

"I have t' get back," John said. He held out his hand. "Good-bye."

Hannah took his hand. Coal grit pressed against her skin. "Watch out for yourself," she said, looking in his face. Then added, as if to clear up any doubt. "You're my friend."

John nodded, "You're mine too." He squeezed her hand, then released it. "Breakfast break'll be over in a minute. I'll head back now."

He left quickly, and Gregory's mother stepped in to the place where he had stood. "I wish we were goin' as well," she sighed. "I don't know what Gregory'll do here. An' I've got another two even younger than him. I can't bear the thought of them in the tunnels." She clutched Maggie's elbow. "Sometimes just knowin' someone makes it easier t' go, though, doesn't it."

"It does," Maggie agreed. She looked at Robbie. "You've been a good friend, Robbie. We'd have been in trouble without you." She patted his hand and bolstered Winnie on her shoulder. It had been a wonder to see this little daughter, red-cheeked and healthy, with the unmistakable dark eyes that all of her daughters had. Maggie looked at her girls. They had found a way to endure, each one of them, through a year of hardship and uncertainty. She felt blessed.

Robbie turned to Hannah. "Grace brought me somethin' that fell out of your shirt. Don't know how you managed it, but I'll get the bow to Ev'lyn some way or other." He shook his head. "Impatient an' pig-headed to a fault." He folded her in his arms. "That's my girl, don't change too much." He stepped away. "I'm off. Don't like seeing friends ride away."

Gregory tapped Hannah on the shoulder as she bent to pick up her basket. "Write me, will y'?"

"Write me back, eh?" She looked at him, then looked away. His mouth was smiling, but his eyes were serious. Putting on a brave front. Her expression was probably the same, she thought.

The train cast its shadow over the platform and crept to a stop. Hannah and Gregory clasped hands. "Gregory, I left the sap pail out back for you. Take it when y' go collectin' sugar from the trees." They both laughed, and it made it easier to let go of each other's hands and turn away.

The girls hung out the window as the wheels moved forward. Gregory and his mother slid by, their faces turned to follow the train. Robbie had stayed through the last farewell. He waved and kept his long arms straight up in the air until the train grew small.

Hannah could see the entire settlement from the station: Robbie's shop, the blond spire of the new church, the forests, the path where her father came home, the blackened hills and the mouth of the mine, and, on the road in the distance, she saw John waving his cap and dancing, his body too big for its years doing a light, slippery jig on the icy road.

Hannah had done what everyone said she couldn't, and she was going away to a new future. John's hopes were bolstered by her success. If she had a future, then so did he.

He saw her lean so far out of the train window he wondered how she didn't fall out, and wave, wave with her whole body.

About the Author

DIANA VAZQUEZ studied film and video at the Ontario College of Art and has spent several years writing and producing her own short independent dramas and experimental films. *Hannah* is her first book publication.

Born in Germany, to Israeli and Spanish parents, Diana Vazquez moved many times with her family before settling in Canada. Her passion for reading sustained her through these many disruptions. The birth of her own daughter in 1988 sparked her interest in writing books for children.